Charles Clarke

Charlie Thornhill; or, the Dunce of the Family

A Novel: Vol. II.

Charles Clarke

Charlie Thornhill; or, the Dunce of the Family
A Novel: Vol. II.

ISBN/EAN: 9783337250287

Printed in Europe, USA, Canada, Australia, Japan

Cover: Foto ©Andreas Hilbeck / pixelio.de

More available books at **www.hansebooks.com**

CHARLIE THORNHILL;

or,

THE DUNCE OF THE FAMILY.

A Novel.

BY

CHARLES CLARKE.

IN THREE VOLUMES.
VOL. II.

LONDON:
CHAPMAN AND HALL, 193, PICCADILLY.
1863.

LONDON:
BRADBURY AND EVANS, PRINTERS, WHITEFRIARS.

CONTENTS.

CONTENTS.

CHARLIE THORNHILL.

CHAPTER I.

AN EVENING IN SHOREDITCH.

"In counsel it is good to see dangers : and in execution not
to see them, except they be very great."—*Bacon's Essays.*

THERE is no doubt that Charlie was in a fix.
Dark as it was, he saw it in that light; and
though bold as a lion, he was by no means as
formidable in this den of wild beasts, whither he
had been led partly by an anxious wish to recover
a very great favourite, and quite as much by a
spirit of adventure, which always had charms for
him, even as a boy.

I always notice that whenever any great rascality has to be committed, or any particularly
criminal mystery has to be solved, the chief
actor invariably whistles. I do not think it
makes less noise than any other mode of sig-

nalling a brother rascal, and it certainly produces an unnecessary action on the nervous system of the victim. There may be something in the old Latin grammar adaptation of Sallust, "Quod factu fædum est, idem turpe est dictu;" and whistling may get over an ethical difficulty. For my own part I see no good in it at all. It only tends to waken suspicion and create alarm; and I would strongly advise all rogues to "keep their own breath to cool their own porridge."

Perhaps the interesting ruffian, who was remarkable for nothing but his handsome, though evil countenance, a certain air of command, and a manifest self-esteem well calculated to impose upon the lower orders of felons, who had brought our hero into this dilemma, was of the same opinion; for having closed the door, and finding himself involved in total darkness, he began to shout with a very audible voice, and no measured language, a demand for a light. "Now then, old Mother Skinflint, how long are we to be kept without a glim? What's become of the lamp?" This demand produced an effect. A door in the wall, on the left, half way down the passage, opened, and disclosed a head more hideous than

anything that Charlie had as yet seen. A scarlet
kerchief surmounted a dark brown wig, at this
time awry, and settling gradually over one of two
eyes as bright and black and piercing as the
other was bleared and innocent of vision. The
face was sharp and hook-nosed, and the mouth
gave visible tokens of the inroads of time. The
lamp was held above her head, and as Charlie
moved towards the door he had time to note
these circumstances of personal appearance. Following his conductor, who steered by the light
ahead, he found himself at once in a large but
dirty kitchen, where a girl, evidently of gipsy
blood, was frying eggs in a large frying-pan,
whilst an unconcerned spectator, with a bridle in
one hand and a heavy jockey-whip in the other,
sat smoking his pipe in the chimney corner.
The windows were strongly barred, and an old
flint and steel gun, hanging at the roof, seemed
the only ostensible means of defence. Opposite
the fire, although a warm night in July, lay
a ferocious-looking mastiff, active, sullen, and
brindled. He showed his teeth at the new arrival, but resumed his couchant attitude at a sign
from the conductor of the party.

Charlie began to be assured, for though several sentences passed between the woman and the guide in a tongue quite incomprehensible to him, still there seemed to be no unfriendly feeling towards the new comer. The girl, indeed, by a natural instinct, made way for him at the fire, though so warm, and he, by an equally natural instinct, smiled and thanked her as he declined the offered place. "If you'll let me," said he, "I'll light my cigar." Saying which, he took his case from his pocket, selected one with considerable care, and proceeded to smoke whilst waiting for further orders from his mysterious conductor.

"Now, if you please," at last said that functionary. "If you'll follow me I'll see what can be done. I suppose that's not the dog?" pointing to the one at the fire. Charlie could not help remarking that the man seldom made a mistake in speaking; and though his manner was utterly without respect for Charlie's condition, and he assumed at least an equality with him throughout, he was free from that coarseness of expression or tone which is almost invariable, in one way or the other, with a man of that class. To Charlie, too, he had made use of no slang expression : his conversation with the old woman was evidently a language, and not thieves' *patter;* and he rightly conjectured that he was in a gipsy's London crib. This reassured him again : for he reflected that if they were the least scrupulous, they had some redeeming qualities of generosity and courage. His was a race-course experience of that remarkable people. He saw the holiday side of them; and he forgot that if they had a negative feeling of good-will to himself, they were actuated by a positive feeling of regard for dogs and money, and would go any length to serve their purpose when safe from detection.

At the further end of the kitchen, and away from the front of the house, as it appeared, was another door. Through this they disappeared, and descending four steps, they made their way, by help of a reflector in the wall, along a second passage of about five-and-twenty feet long to a room apparently detached from the kitchen. The door opened with an ordinary latch. By the very recent smell of tobacco-smoke it had been lately occupied, and a rough arm-chair, one of the only pieces of furniture in the room, retained the impression of a late sitter. There

was a rough round table retaining the marks of
pewter pots in full force, and a torn copy of
"Bell's Life," some weeks old, had found its
way into this den of thieves. The room itself
was of good size, some twenty-five feet by twenty.
Over a battered-looking chimney-piece, now un-
used as a grate, there was a likeness of the
celebrated buggy horse "Coventry, the property
of Lord Ongley;" and round the room were
some villanously - coloured engravings of celebrated pugilists. A set of gloves in one corner
bespoke the occupation of leisure hours, and
some strong staples let into the wall here and
there looked like "baiting." In fact, it was a
convenient place for the commission of iniquities,
or for the promotion of sports peculiar to certain
classes, and might be the scene of a murder or
Sabbath-day's recreation for the neighbours, as
the case might be. Charlie was allowed full
leisure for the examination of the chamber, and
for reflections upon his folly in coming to it.
He lifted up a dim light, afforded by a bad
rushlight in a sconce, and examined the like-
nesses of Molyneux, Dutch Sam, Sambo Sutton,
White-headed Bob, and the aforesaid Coventry.

The chair was too dirty to sit down in, and the literary remains too filthy to read. A chorus of dogs, manifestly close at hand, kept breaking upon the ear, and the occasional clanking of a chain, and a rate, accompanied by a deep curse, reminded him of his errand. Surely that was his old favourite Rose. He went to a barred shutter and listened. Somebody was quieting her, and loosing the chain from a staple in the kennel or wall to which she was fastened. In another minute he heard a smothered conversation: it sounded like a dispute. Then he heard steps of heavy boots, not as if intended for concealment, and immediately after a heavy door, which was on the opposite side of the room from that by which Charlie had entered, opened slowly, and a man made his appearance, leaving the door partially open, however, as though for communication, or more comers. As he advanced into the room Charlie saw a face which seemed not entirely unknown to him. It had gipsy blood stamped on it, with the peculiar fire of the eyes of that people. But it had none of their beauty, for the other natural lineaments of the face were disfigured, swollen, and flattened

by the exercise of the calling to which he manifestly belonged—that of a fighter. He was a
hard-set man of about thirty-five, and had lost
some of the activity and wire of youth. In his
best days, science being equal, he would not
have been a match for Charlie. He had neither
his reach nor size across the chest, his length of
limb, nor fine clean hips, indicative of activity.
The measurement Charlie took of him was satisfactory, as the two men eyed one another—
tolerably good specimens of their class, but the
gentleman, even in mere *physique*, bearing the
bell.

After a dogged silence of about a minute, the
man addressed him.

"You're come about a dog?"

"I am," said Charlie Thornhill.

"What sort do you want?"

"A white bull bitch, very handsome, and highly
bred —almost thorough-bred, but with a grey-
hound mouth. She answers to the name of Rose."

"I dessay she do. Leastways, I haven't tried
her. We don't know anything about names here.
You call her what you please. We've got a very
nice 'un."

"Can I see her?" said Charlie, re-lighting his cigar, which he had allowed to go out.

"Oh! yes, certainly; she's a very nice 'un, mind ye; she's a gentleman's dawg all over;" which was equivalent to admitting that she belonged to no one in Shoreditch, at all events. "Here, Bill," said he, "bring in the little bitch, you know, as we got for the sporting sugar-baker in Whitechapel."

Bill was not long in responding. A chain was heard, and in rushed Rose, dragging Bill after her, and making her way at once to Charlie Thornhill with every demonstration of satisfaction. "Rose, Rose; down Rose; be quiet, good bitch; down," said he. And she stood looking up at her master with every limb like alabaster.

"Well! I suppose you're convinced she's my dog?" said Charlie.

"We never asks any questions about whose dog she is, when she comes into our hands. We supposes as you wants to buy a dog like this 'un here," said the man, quietly leading her away and fastening her by her chain to a staple in the wall at the other end of the room. "We'd as lief sell her to you as to any one else."

This was putting a virtuous aspect on a nefarious transaction : clothing poverty in fine linen
with a vengeance.   However, that was their look-
out, and Charlie saw nothing very much to object
to in this flimsy veil of honesty.   The sight of
the dog, too, had sharpened his appetite for his
property, so he replied very simply—

"Then I should like to buy the bitch.   I'm
given to understand that three pounds——"

"Three pounds ?   Lor ! there's hundreds as 'ud
give twenty.   You can't buy a hanimal like this
here for twice three pounds, not if she wur stole."

Charlie was losing patience.   "D——n your
impudence !   Why, she *was* stolen.   She belongs
to me, I tell you.   What do you suppose I came
here for : to buy my own property again at its
full value ?"

"I don't know anything about that," said the
man, sulkily, "but I ain't a going to part with
that dog under twice three pounds; so if you
ain't a mind to give more, there's an end of the
deal."

During the whole of this time Rose kept on
whining significantly, standing at the full length
of her chain, and straining her eyes and limbs

in the direction of Charlie. He was becoming more determined than ever to repossess himself of his property, and the impudence of the robbery added fuel to the flame.

" Then you don't mean to give me back my dog ? "

" I don't mean to sell this here bitch for less than six pounds."

" " There are the three sovereigns," and Charlie placed them in the palm of his hand, where they glittered temptingly in the surrounding gloom.

" They're no use : put 'em up again ; why the collar's pretty nigh worth the money," and he pointed to a handsomely-worked steel collar, which had either never been removed, or was now replaced.

" Why ! you infernal scoundrel, there's my own name on it ! I insist upon having the dog," saying which, with a firmly-closed lip, and a heavy determined step, Charlie moved towards the dog.

But the gipsy anticipated his movement, and was there before him.

" Stand on one side." The man put himself into a posture of defence, and struck rapidly out ;

but Charlie stopped the blow with his left arm, and closed with him at once. Up to that moment Rose had been quiet enough: with the instinct peculiar to all the bull-dog kind, she no sooner heard the shuffling of feet, than her whole nature changed. She sprang violently to the length of her chain; she strained every muscle in her endeavours to free herself; her mouth foamed, her prominent eyes became bloodshot, and her short bark changed into a prolonged and fearful yell. The chain almost yielded to her efforts, as she fell at each bound in her frantic struggles back upon the floor. Charlie in the mean time had seized the neckcloth of his antagonist with his left hand, and his left wrist with his right. The struggle would not have been long, had they been left to themselves; already he was dragging him towards the dog, who would soon have declared for her master, when he saw the gipsy's disengaged hand descend rapidly into his shooting-coat pocket, and reappear with a glistening knife. Nothing remained to be done but to release his throat and get possession of the other hand. In a moment he had done so; but in that moment the man sent forth a shout for

help, to which the hurry of steps told of a re-
sponse. At the same instant, changing his right
hand from the wrist to the throat, and placing
his leg rapidly behind him, Charlie threw him
on the back of his head within reach of Rose.
The dog seized him by the throat, whilst the
frantic efforts of the gipsy were unavailing to free
himself from the powerful gripe of our hero.
Charlie dared not let go; the life of his dog
would have been the forfeit. Easing himself,
therefore, he placed his knee upon the fallen
man's chest, bent upon forcing the weapon from
him, when with a loud bang the door flew open,
and he was seized by the collar from behind.
Matters looked serious; he remembered his
whistle, and his life-preserver. Relaxing his
hold of the throat, and resisting the violent
efforts that were being made to disengage him
from behind, he dragged them from a side pocket
of the old paletot with which he had endeavoured
to conceal his respectability. One shrill blast,
which startled both his assailants for a second,
and one gentle blow on the arm above the wrist,
which dropped the armed limb as though it had
been broken, released him from his prostrate foe.

He turned rapidly in his kneeling posture upon
the ruffian who held him from behind, and at the
same moment his conductor appeared upon the
stage from the other door. "Hold hard," said
he in a voice of authority, which so paralyzed the
powerful fellow who still grappled with Charlie,
that he was enabled to rise. Close on his foot-
steps followed the Léonarde of the establishment,
and as the only truly dangerous member was still
under the fangs of the dog, the affray was almost
terminated. Fear kept the prisoner quiet. The
conductor approached the dog and was met with
a low growl.

"Call off the dog, in God's name."

"That's not so easy to do; besides which, your
comrade has another hand at liberty, and a
drawn knife by his side; one arm is disabled; if
he moves the other," said Charlie, "I can't be
answerable for the consequences. The quieter
he lies the better for him." With that he picked
up the knife. The old woman went to the fallen
man. "What, Giles, not blood enough yet!"
Giles held his tongue, almost his breath. Rose
showed no inclination to let go.

"Call off the dog, if you can do so. Lie still,

Giles," said the black-haired conductor, who had a curious expression of sadness stealing over his handsome features. And Charlie went to Rose, and loosed the chain. With a few words he soothed the dog, which after a low growl or two retired to his heels, and the fallen man got on his legs.

"There, Giles, take your three sovereigns, and let him have his dog; give him the three sovereigns. See him safe through the ·kitchen, mother. I owe him a life and I pay it. Take your dog, and be gone. Do you know your way?"

"Am I safe?" said Charlie, who began to realize the dangers of his exploit, as he handed over the three sovereigns.

"Yes; and if you're stopped before you get into the main street the sign is 'Cast off.' You're a gentleman—promise on your word of honour not to betray us. Your dog is safe, for us, for the future."

"I do promise;" and having leisurely brushed his hat with his sleeve, and shaken the dust from his clothes, he followed the old woman, with Rose at his heels, from the scene of his recent struggle.

It has taken a long time in telling, but the encounter scarcely lasted as many seconds as there are lines in the recital.

Once outside the felon's haunt, he traversed the alleys with rapid strides, doubtful whether, when he regained the street, he should find his cab. He was not long in uncertainty; he was still some hundred yards from the "Lively Fleas," which seemed to be driving a roaring trade, when he met his cab, coming slowly towards him. The man recognised him in an instant; he jumped in without a word, followed by the dog, and about five-and-forty minutes or something more saw him at the top of Grosvenor Place. It was now eleven o'clock, and having paid his charioteer handsomely and returned him his property, he strolled quietly down to his mother's door.

CHAPTER II.

THE END OF THE SEASON.

"Fire that is closest kept, burns most of all."
Two Gentlemen of Verona.

"WHERE are you going, Charlie? I hear you have given orders for packing up; is it to Scotland?" said Mrs. Thornhill, on the morning following Charlie's desperate adventure. Circumstances made him look grave; and Mary Stanhope was fond of thinking that he did not take sufficient care of himself. They were two devoted women; and the large black eyes and sallow skin of Aunt Mary concealed a whole ocean of love for the brothers, which was always overflowing in one way or another, sometimes in praise, as often in censure.

"No, my dear mother; but if you will have me for a month at Thornhills, I should like to go down. I've nothing between that and the Rhine, until September," said her son. "I am going to Bognor for the Goodwood week ; Tom's gone."

"And where do you go in September ? I thought the shooting at Thornhills was good enough to tempt any one."

"To the Dacres : Tom won't be at home; he never begins till nearly the middle of the month, and then the house will be full."

"I thought you liked a full house."

"So he does, Emily," said Aunt Mary, "but he's going to look after Tom's interests. There are two sisters you know, Charlie, and I prefer the eldest myself; so take care of yourself. When do the Dacres leave town ?"

"To-morrow. You're curious, Aunt Mary."

"Sign of an inquiring mind, Charlie; you've no curiosity, and that's why you are so idle."

"I never trouble myself about other people's business."

"Thank you, Charlie—I do; and it's very fortunate for you and your dear mother that I have the taste for it; I don't know what would become of you all. So now tell me, where are the Dacres going ? to Gilsland ?"

"No, to some people near Chichester for Goodwood, called the Robinson Browns."

"Do you know who the Robinson Browns are, Charlie?"

"No, thank goodness; but probably you do, Aunt Mary."

"Yes, I do know something about them; I wonder a man like Mr. Dacre should take his wife and daughters there. Robinson Brown indeed! What a name it is."

"It's a very good name in its way. He's not a Stanhope; but he has large houses, fine horses, magnificent plate, loads of ready money, and a large establishment," said Charlie, with a sinister smile.

"And large daughters and plenty of them," added Mary Stanhope, with considerable energy, "whom Mrs. Robinson Brown wishes to marry to the best men in town. Do you call that reputable, Charlie?"

"Well! It's the way of the world."

"I hope your wife won't do so, whenever you have one. Your mother, poor thing, is saved from the temptation. I shouldn't have been much use to her here." And, true enough, she

would not. Your matchmaker wants a very
peculiar combination of qualities—a mind capable of very well-disguised dissimulation, and
guided by a principle of lying upon occasion,
which would have gladdened the heart of the
great Lord Shaftesbury; a disinterestedness
which covets all things, and an innocent sim-
plicity of character all but omniscient; Argus-
like blindness; great self-restraint; a taste for
everything, especially manly pursuits and clas-
sical erudition, combined with an incapacity for
physical exertion most opportune; an infallible
knowledge of an elder son, or an eligible *parti*;
a close acquaintance with the Peerage and
Baronetage, and Burke's Landed Gentry; and a
capability for absorbing, or radiating, warmth as
occasion demands; great affection—for herself
and her young; much courage—in repelling the
advances of a detrimental; and steadiness in
the pursuit of her game, which is supposed only
to belong to the bloodhound on the track of the
fugitive slave. If to all these you add great
knowledge of gastronomy, discernment of affini-
ties and combination, delicacy of touch, so as
not to alarm the timid, tenacity of purpose, so

as not to let go the captive, and a veil of fascination over the whole character which reminds of the last scene of a pantomime, or a poached egg in pea-soup, and you have our friend Mrs. Robinson Brown as clearly as if Frank Grant himself had drawn the picture.

Beyond this there was no harm in Mrs. Robinson Brown and her daughters. Mary Stanhope was a prejudiced old woman. She was not unlike one half of her own acquaintance. She had the misfortune to be of the *aucune famille*, and to have the revenues of a duchess, or she might have pursued her schemes without remark. Besides her daughters, however, whom she destined to get off, she had a son who had made up his mind to be guided by nothing but taste in the choice of a wife. This young gentleman had hit upon Edith Dacre, as combining all advantages but one, that of money, and which deficiency he proposed himself to supply. Hence the pressing invitation to the Dacres to join their Goodwood party; and as they were really people who went everywhere, and knew everybody, there seemed no difficulty in accepting.

Anybody at all versed in old-maidenism will see with half an eye that Mary Stanhope—and I call her so, for I never heard her called Miss Stanhope by any one but the servants—was as good a soul as ever lived. She had that little vice, which on certain occasions exalts itself into a virtue, and which we have already noticed, curiosity; but her motives were so good, that nobody who knew her ever called her inquisitions in question. They were not always convenient, it is true, and might have something vague about them to the general listener; but she had a reason of her own for most things that she said and did, and it not unfrequently became apparent when least expected. The day before Charlie's departure for Bognor, she sat for some time evidently big with thought, and plied her knitting, the only work she condescended to engage in—fine, strong, warm, Welsh-woollen socks for her boys for the shooting season.

"Charlie, do you know a man I can depend upon to do a commission for me?" said the lady.

"Very few; but it depends upon what it is. Shall I do?" said the gentleman.

"No, not you; you know I never ask irrelevant questions. Is your friend Mr. Cressingham still in town?"

"I believe he is; why?"

"Well! I like the look of him better than De Beauvoir or Mr. Dacre."

"De Beauvoir's an ass; Teddy's not a bad fellow, but scarcely to be depended upon for business. Won't the family lawyer, old Mr. Sharpus, do?"

"Certainly not; he's no better than I am myself—an honest old woman."

"Then it must be Cressingham. If I can find him at the club this morning I'll bring him here. Aunt Mary, you're a regular Œdipus."

"If Lady Elizabeth heard that, she'd say *you* were no conjuror; Sphinx, I suppose you mean; you're the Œdipus, you know."

"Ah, well! good morning; I never was much of a hand at that sort of thing; I'll bring Cressingham back to lunch."

No sooner was Charlie Thornhill gone than Mary Stanhope was once more interrupted. Fortunately, knitting is not like the throes of composition, and will bear interruption. I have

often imagined that it acts almost like a sedative;
and rather strengthens for the infliction, or
enables to bear with patience, what to an utterly
idle or thoroughly busy mind might be an infliction. Mrs. Thornhill opened the door, and
occupied her younger son's vacant seat. As she
had the " Times " in her hand, you may be quite
sure she came for conversation. Whenever I
see a person seize the newspaper, and retire
doggedly to a distant arm-chair, or to his own
room, I know he or she means reading; but
when I see them come into a room, already
occupied, from another part of the house, newspaper in hand, I always assume that they mean
talking, and prepare myself accordingly. A
large sheet like the " Times " covers a multitude
of sins.

" Mary," said Mrs. Thornhill, spreading the
paper upside down, and staring silently at it so
as to hide her face, " what's the matter with
Charlie ? "

" Nothing at all, my dear, that I can see ; he
looks well enough."

" Oh ! yes ; but he talks of reading for some
examination, either for the army or for some

government appointment; and he has ordered his horses to be sold. I'm sure he'll make himself ill."

"The most useful thing he has done, my dear, for years. Don't be at all alarmed about Charlie." Miss Stanhope liked nobody to spoil him but herself. "I thought it was Tom you came to talk about." This was a fib; but certain authorities have dealt very leniently with this vice, so that lying, upon occasion, becomes almost commendable.

"Tom! oh no, poor dear Tom," said the widow, with one of her sweetest smiles, and a not very deep sigh, "he has but one fault."

"Yes; and that one leads to everything bad, and will end in utter ruin. Speak to him about his play before it's too late, Emily."

"_I_ speak to Tom about his gambling!"

"Yes, you; who so fit as a mother? if he won't attend to you, do you think he will pay attention to me?"

"I'm sure he would," said the poor weak woman, "he's so affectionate; oh! if he would but marry." Mrs. Thornhill believed matrimony to be a sort of panacea—a Morison's pill-box

made palatable. As to any young lady swal-
lowing it, gilded with her son, no difficulty
presented itself to her.

"And who would you like him to marry?"
Mary Stanhope, you see, had never learnt the
Latin grammar; but the fact is, that so few
people of condition do speak correctly, that we
authors are considerably posed. "There's Julia
Brown Smith—oh! Robinson Brown, is it? well,
I'm always making mistakes about names, Emily,
I know; but I can't help it. She's just as
extravagant as he is, and hasn't half his sense.
Then there's Lady Caroline Lambkin; a sick
wife to nurse: he'd become more selfish than
ever."

"I'm sure he's not selfish, Mary; he's the
most liberal, kind-hearted, generous——"

"Yes, dear, but not self-denying; and there's
a great deal of difference between the two." It's
astonishing how sensibly she could talk, and how
foolishly she could act, upon occasion. She had
petted and spoiled Tom; had given him all she
could scrape together out of her own privy purse;
had encouraged his extravagance at Eton; and
had never contradicted him, excepting in trifles,

and then only out of opposition. When a boy, she had bought him cigars, which he was forbidden to smoke; she sent him money to pay his childish debts of honour, when his father had refused the application; and then he, in the end, usually got both. Even now, if anybody but herself had suggested that he required correction, she would have put herself into a violent ill-humour, and refused to believe one word to his prejudice. "Then there's that Miss Dacre, the pretty one, that we see everywhere."

"Well, now, Mary, what do you think of her? he's going there this season."

"Oh! she's well enough; but she's flighty: she's no stability, not an atom; no more stability than a cat upon walnut-shells. Her sister's worth a dozen of her; the one that came to the Carnabys with Lady Elizabeth what's her name? an antediluvian sort of name."

"Mastodon, Mary; that's the name. If he'd only fall in love with somebody, I should be satisfied. As to Charlie, there are no hopes of him."

"That's a comfort; he'd better learn to keep himself before he thinks of a wife. He'll fall

in love quite soon enough for his own good, and
somebody else's too." Miss Stanhope chose to
consider that she had had a disappointment
early in life.

All good things come round at last, and of
course luncheon - time with everything else.
When a man has a luncheon to go to, there's
scarcely anything pleasanter, excepting breakfast
and dinner. It's only convenience is that you
can cut it when you please. Women never do cut
it; it is as essential to them as a labourer's
eleven o'clock, or his after-dinner pipe—not of
wine. One of the accidents of luncheon to-day
was the arrival of Mr. Cressingham, who, contrary to his wont—such is the force of example
—ate a cutlet, some plum-pudding fried in slices,
orange cream, a slice of cake, and finished with
no end of brown sherry. I have no doubt it
was all distasteful to him, but every man does
it when he has nothing else to do. What gor-
mandizers two-thirds of the men in London
ought to be, say you; *au contraire*, their minds are
so occupied with what they shall eat for dinner,
that they can scarcely be said to be unemployed.
At length the last vestige of the meal was re-

moved, and when the ladies ought to have gone up-stairs Miss Stanhope remained behind. Cressingham had received orders, and lingered about the door, which Charlie deliberately shut in his face.

"Mr. Cressingham," said Aunt Mary, not having the slightest idea that she bored the man to death, "I want you to do a commission for me; I cannot do it for myself, and when I say horseflesh is concerned, you will understand that I am in a dilemma, or something of that sort you call it."

Cressingham suggested "a fix."

"Of course, that's what I meant to say, 'a regular fix.' You know Charlie has taken to reading, and I'm sure it will injure his health, so I——"

"Permit me, Miss Stanhope," said Cressingham, "Charlie has not taken to reading, and I don't think he will injure his health."

"Do you know that his horses are to be sold?"

"Yes, Miss Stanhope, next Monday—one's a beauty."

"Is that his favourite?"

" Yes, it is: I don't know the price put upon the horse, but I should have thought twice about selling him."

"Will you buy him, Mr. Cressingham?" said Miss Stanhope, eagerly.

"Well, that's not precisely the same thing, you know. A man may not be obliged to part with what he has, though he may not be in a position to buy what he'd like to have. No, I can't buy him."

"Could you buy him for a friend without letting Charles Thornhill know anything about it?" said Miss Stanhope, again.

"Yes," said Cressingham, dragging out his words deliberately, "I could do so, of course: but he would know some time or other who had him; he's too good, Miss Stanhope, to be kept under a bushel."

"Under a good many bushels," said the lady, who was very matter of fact, and whose head was running upon the corn-bin; "but could you buy him for a friend, at a fair price, without letting the name transpire?"

"I must, in fact, buy him in my own name; that's easy enough."

"Do as you please about that; but I wish to buy him. Will you do this commission for me?" It was out at last.

"Certainly, I will ascertain the reserved price, and see what can be done to get him for you at as little money as possible."

"Don't do that, Charlie will get the money; don't let him lose a shilling by the transaction, whatever you do. Only let me be the purchaser; and, though I am a very economical person, I shouldn't like it to go into any other hands. I really feel exceedingly obliged to you, Mr. Cressingham."

"All right, Miss Stanhope, your commission shall be done; shall I send him to your London stables or to Thornhills?"

"Oh! to Thornhills, if you please," said Miss Stanhope. "We shall be gone from here in another week at the latest; if I give you a blank cheque signed to fill up——"

"No, no, Miss Stanhope; that's too great a temptation: wait till you have the horse, or know that you are to have him: I'll arrange the cheque, and let you know the price in good time." After a few minutes more of unimportant conversation, Cressingham took his leave.

Of all the race-courses in England, there's nothing like Goodwood; and of all the empty-headed idiots that were to be found there at the end of July, 18—, there was no one equal to Mr. Robinson Brown, junior. Newmarket is, as a mere race-course, of course unapproachable. As a matter of business, of profit,—as the *pied à terre* of the wealthy turfite, the ardent sports-man, or the legitimate betting-man,—there can be no comparison with any other place. Epsom has a hill, and a race which carries the blue riband of the turf with it; but it has a London mob, and the transport of all the riot and drunkenness of England from its provincial dens to the hill; and the grandeur of the Derby is lost in the profligacy of a public Saturnalia. Ascot has its royalty, its carriages, and its Grand Stand—a terrible drawback to its former visible elegance, when dukes and marquises, with ladies fair and noble, encountered between the races the work-a-day world of men and women out for a holiday-making; and instead of an indis-tinguishable mass of beauty, colour, whisker,

and *épicierism bien gantée*, we saw form and
fashion from head to foot as it is and was,
but as it seldom could be seen elsewhere by the
dingy votaries of the unprivileged class. Don-
caster boasts a St. Leger and "t'Coop," with
its proud old county families, and ancestral
carriages, its Yorkshire tykeism, and its enthu-
siastic partisanship; but there is but one course
that unites sport, beauty, fashion, and the
picturesque, without any alloy of dust, or smoke,
or riot, or degradation—a scene which Watteau
could have painted, or Boccaccio have sung in
all its integrity—and that is Goodwood. Its
sloping lawn, how charming! where beneath the
shadow of that magnificent belt of trees lie the
loveliest women in the world, bright, sparkling,
in a mixture of floods of light, and iced champagne, gorgeous in jewellery and toilette, or
simplices munditiis, and conquering by the unsuspected nature of their unadorned loveliness.
Here and there in attendance, are grouped the
knightly cavalier of modern growth; watchful of
his mistress's unexpressed wants, and ready to
enhance the pleasures of a brilliant holiday
by cheerful solicitude for her happiness. The

undulating expanse of park land, studded with
noble trees, and sweetened by the breath of the
southern coast breeze, with the excitement of
the pastime, the ostensible motive of the visit,
add a charm to Goodwood, which must be ex-
perienced to be understood.

As usual, all the world was to be there. I
mean, of course, the few thousands of happy
mortals who put in a claim for that distinction.
Out of that world there could have been no
existence for Mr. John Robinson Brown ; or,
as he was more commonly known in his regi-
ment, " dear Jane," or the " Heir Apparent," the
latter sobriquet having been obtained from the
preposterous exhibition of jewellery upon his
person.

How he came to be Robinson Brown is simple enough. The Robinsons were respectable
miners ; that is, the grandfather and granduncles
of " dear Jane." They amassed wealth by
wholesome toil, unvarying honesty, an intelligence superior to their *confrères*, and undeviating
luck. From excavating the ground when soft,
and from blasting it when hard, from the pick
and the borer, they raised themselves gradually,

at a time when some mechanical knowledge was exceedingly valuable. They became tenants in fee simple of some land which proved considerably more productive beneath its surface than upon it, and the wealth of the three brothers centred at length in the only heir, the father of Mr. John Robinson Brown. A long minority added to his already ample fortune; of him might be truly quoted the lines of Horace, with a pardonable second intention :—

> " Illi robur et *æs triplex*
> Circa pectus erat."

His soul was steeled with threefold gold; Mr. Robinson was one of the hardest, richest, and vulgarest men alive. He was essentially a man of a vulgar mind. His wealth had brought him education at Harrow and Oxford, his incapability for the ordinary accomplishments of a country gentleman had given him his only redeeming qualification, a fondness for books; not poor men's books, but expensive mediæval manuscripts, and richly-bound rarities, which could excite the appetite of the truly learned or the hereditarily noble. He had the same taste for furniture. A drawing-room paper was only valuable as it gave an opportunity for exposing the cost, at eight shillings a yard; and a picture was estimable by its capacity for depth of frame. At this time, as a young man, he married—not a woman, but money. Miss Brown, of Manchester, was undistinguishable save as the niece of the richest of cotton-spinners; a good man, a clever man, but proud of the name and honest industry by which civic honours, wealth, and reputation had belonged to three generations of Browns. Mr. Brown knew nothing of his nephew-in-law; but when he died he left his fortune, without his character, to his niece's husband, upon condition that he added the name of Brown to his own. It would have been better had it been Howard or Neville; but he went to bed one night Robinson, with five hundred thousand, and rose the next morning Brown, with a million of money to his name.

Robinson Brown had since then cultivated the peerage; and he loved a lord not for the good he did, but for what he was. His house was full of them now, and amongst his favoured guests came the Dacres. He had seen, perhaps,

his own mistake in wedding a Miss Brown of
Manchester, and he was anxious to remedy the
defect in his son. His pride of purse was so
great that he rather preferred a portionless girl,
to whose dazzled senses the brightness of his
money might be the more apparent. So he held
divers conversations with Mrs. Robinson Brown,
who pumped her son very satisfactorily, and it
seemed to be a settled affair between father,
mother, and son, that the latter should endow
one of the Misses Dacre of Gilsland, a Talbot
and a Greystock, with the ample resources and
inane insipidity of a Robinson Brown.

Under the aforesaid trees in Goodwood there
was, amongst other gay and happy parties, a
circle as gay and as happy as any. Robinson
Brown, to do him justice, had given every facility
to his guests for enjoying themselves. All that
excellent cookery, and the best champagne, well
iced, could do had been done. The weather,
too, was propitious; and some of his friends had
won a good stake or two. The selection of
women did Mrs. Robinson Brown great credit.
They were very good-looking, distinguées, and
had been got together without any of that jealousy

which would have excluded rivalry to the Brown
girls.   Alice and Edith Dacre looked positively
lovely.   Tom Thornhill had just come back to
the Stand, and was receiving the congratulations
of his friends on having won a good handicap.
Charlie was seated on a drag just outside the
rails of the lawn, and dividing his attention between cold pie and champagne and the Robinson
Brown party.

" Charlie, who's that talking to Dacre's sister,
with lots of harness—jewellery, I mean : the man
with lank whiskers, and looking generally washed
out ? "

"Don't you know?   Why the biggest fool in
England—Robinson Brown."

" Don't say so ? that's the ' Heir Apparent,'
is it ? he's a very good-looking one."

" Oh ! come, nonsense, Truffles, you know
better than that."

" And there's your brother Tom : The Plunger
doesn't show quite so well by the side of him ;
he's talking to the other Miss Dacre. What
a pity they have no money. Had your brother
backed his filly for anything ? "

" Thornhill," said a jovial-looking young man,

from the wheel of the drag, "come into the Stand a minute, that's a good fellow."

"What is it?" said Charlie, lighting a cigar at the same moment.

"They're talking about a match between one of your brother's hunters and a horse of ' dear Jane's ;' they want to know if you'll ride, so come down."

Charlie had been vacillating for some time between a little fit of the sulks and his wish to join the party with whom his brother was now talking. He knew most of them well ; but the Dacres frightened him : and he saw neither Lady Marston, nor Lady Elizabeth Montagu Mastodon. But for this friendly chance of cutting-in, he must have left Mr. Robinson Brown master of the position. He slowly descended from the drag, stood ten minutes smoking and talking to the ambassador from the lawn, finally threw away his cigar, and without saying a word strode silently off at the back of the trees towards the Stand.

With half a dozen nods to the men whom he knew, and a cheerful five minutes' chat with Lady Marston, whom he met on the way, he joined

the happy group he had been longing to join
for the last two hours.

" We have a match on between your brother's
brown horse and Robinson Brown's mare Reluctance, 12 st., to be run in November, in
Leicestershire or Northamptonshire : will you
ride ? "

Charlie hesitated.

" Do, Mr. Thornhill, I shall back your
brother, if you will ride for him," said Alice
Dacre ; still Charlie hesitated : he wanted a word
or a look from Edith. He did not quite understand why he did not get it. She had shaken
hands with him, and was now apparently listen-
ing to the platitudes of Robinson Brown.

" Oh ! I'm so glad you like steeple-chasing,
Miss Edith, it is so delightful : so much—aw—
aw—fresh air and that sort of thing, you
know."

" Dangerous, I think," said Mrs. Brown.

" Cruel, I fear," said the oldest Miss Brown.

" Do you think it dangerous, Miss Edith ? of
course, you know, naturally—aw—aw—I mean
aw—post and wails, and hairwy ditches, and that
sort of thing. But——"

"Some people's heads are thick enough for anything. I should think there was no harm in your riding, Mr. Brown." Here everybody laughed excepting Brown, who did not seem to know at what they were laughing.

"Oh, no! besides I've widden before, Miss Dacre, and it's quite delightful. Did I win? No, no! I didn't win. I got into the bwook, you know. I got vewy wet; of course I was wet, you know."

"But some people are not born to be drowned, Mr. Brown;" and another cheerful roar greeted this second sally. "And what did you do in the brook?"

"Oh! I stood there and wung——"

"Your hands, I presume," said Lady Elizabeth.

"No, my pocket-handkerchief; it was so vewy uncomfortable; and then the man to whom the horse belonged, a howwid Colonel Somebody, came down and abused me for not winning: he said if I'd only holloed at him, he'd have jumped it like—like anything. But I'd lost all my bweath by the time we came to the water, so of course I couldn't hollo. You know, Miss Dacre, a fellow couldn't hollo without any bweath, could he?"

"Do you intend to ride your brother's horse," said Edith, turning suddenly round upon Charlie Thornhill. "Is he a very good horse? They all think he can win, if you ride him."

Charlie smiled, a happy, pleased smile: it was all he wanted, and said: "Yes, he is a capital horse; he doesn't know how to fall. You had better back him; I think I shall win:" the last *sotto voce*.

"I will back him, and I hope you may." She nodded her head gaily at the same time, and turned to speak to one of the Misses Robinson Brown, who were paying her marked attention.

In the meantime Tom Thornhill had been receiving the congratulations of his friends. He ought to have been a happy man, but he was not. There was one voice, for which he began to care too much, and that had not joined in the general expression of congratulations. Alice Dacre looked grave, and held her peace: Love's eyes are prophetic of danger. She turned to Charlie, and said, "Your brother has won a good deal of money, has he not?"

"I believe so, but I never ask about his betting-book; the stakes are not much." Charlie was always communicative to Alice Dacre.

"Did you bet on the filly he ran?"

"No, Miss Dacre; I never bet, excepting a mere trifle. You know I can't afford it."

"Nobody can afford it, at least if reputation is of any value." Alice Dacre joined to a naturally acute and very truthful mind a great dislike to unequal associations for those she liked; and she heard and saw too much of the evils of the system to shut her eyes to its results. But what was it to her if Tom Thornhill ruined himself body and soul; she had no power to avert it.

CHAPTER III.

OLD ACQUAINTANCE.

"Time is the old justice that examines all offenders."

As You Like It.

THE reading public has a great love for the aristocracy, or authors of the present day are labouring under an error. I dare no more have written of the Smiths, the Joneses, and the Greens, than I could have ventured upon a treatise against mesmeric influence, with the hope of popularity. Nor is it a love for the virtues of the upper classes which awakens this apparent interest in their proceedings. On the contrary, I have rather noticed an anxiety for any description of the frivolities and vices of fashionable society. And certainly there is no lack of writers ready to exhibit their own inti- mate connection with these classes, and who take delight in displaying an acquaintance with folly to which we have no parallel amongst them within my knowledge. The devil is never so black as he is painted; and if in these pages the reader be struck by a more economical use of high-toned vice, and some pictures of its sense and worth, I shall ask him to pause before he sets me down as a flatterer and a sycophant, and to inquire for himself after that wonderful virtue of the middle classes which has been hiding itself under a bushel for some time past. Experience, I think, Fielding declares to be the first of the gifts necessary for the successful development of a story—as needful for the portrayal of a duke as of a prize-fighter, of a duchess as of a scullery-maid. If this be so, I cannot compliment the majority of the caterers for public taste on the society in which they must have passed much of their time, who give to a nobleman or gentleman the principles of a stableman, and to a lady of rank the weakness or heartlessness of a professional profligate.

A few months after the scene at Goodwood, and when the natural fruit of such circumstances had arrived at maturity; that is, when Tom Thornhill had made further inroads on his property, but was as cheerful and happy as ever;

when the fascinating John Robinson Brown
began to speculate on the chances of his success
with Edith Dacre with almost less fear and
trembling than on the event of the match
between Reluctance and the brown horse; when
Alice Dacre had had some practice in steeling ·
her heart against a gambler, and found how
difficult it was to do so; when Edith had had
time to weigh the value of Mr. Robinson Brown's
acres against the honestest but least-confident
love that could be offered her; and when Charlie
himself, finding out the real state of his heart
and pocket, had made up his mind that if work
could win what he most valued on earth, no toil
should deter him from its pursuit; then it was
that Mr. Burke sat patiently in the back office
of a house in the principal street of the city of
Cork. Pleasant images passed through his brain.
He was prosperous, respected, unsuspected; had
a good digestion, and suffered less from conscientious pangs than most men. He had thriven
immensely since the perpetration of his great
rascality. He had possessed himself of the title-
deeds of the little estate belonging to Kildonald
—he had safe in his custody the receipt for the

few thousands of purchase-money for that estate
which had been sent by him to poor Geoffrey
Thornhill, the victim of a mistake, which accident, however, had thus enriched him. The
same channel which carried to him the receipt,
amongst other papers, which happened to be on
his person on the day of the murder, brought
him the betting-book, which was mysteriously
forwarded to Sir Frederick Marston, by which
happy incident his bets were paid. Since that
day, for some reasons, Mr. Burke had confined
his attentions to the sister isle as a betting man,
excepting on some few occasions, by commission,
modestly ignoring the scenes of former triumphs
or reverses. He now sat happy in apparent
prosperity, and in the respect of all good men
and some very bad ones.

His office-door opened, and a shock-headed
Irish clerk appeared with a pen behind his ear
and a sheet of half-copied parchment in his
hand.

"Here's some one to see you, Misther Burke."

"What is his business?" said Mr. Burke.

"It isn't conveyancing, I'll go bail, nor to buy
the Ballymooney estate."

" What's he like ? "

" Faix, he's no beauty then ; but some of us is
none the worse for that." Here Phelim stroked
his own chin, which would have been the better
for a razor.

" Send him in, and be in the way, Phelim,"
and the respectable Mr. Burke put on his
most respectable look. It was rather thrown
away upon the figure that now entered the
room.

A sturdy-looking countryman in a frieze coat,
drab hat, gaiters, a black or dark-brown wig, and
large whiskers of the same colour, stood in the
doorway and looked stealthily round. " May I
come in ? " said he, and without waiting reply, he
turned the lock of the door, and began divesting
himself of his wig and whiskers. Having done
so, he appeared to have light-coloured hair and
red whiskers of no great size ; the change
brought Burke to his feet with a look of
horror.

" In God's name, Mike, where do you come
from ? Do you know your danger, man ? "

" No man better, Mr. Burke, leastways if it's
not yourself. It's a bad boat we've been sailing

in," said the other with a cunning leer; craft was the distinguishing characteristic of his face.

"Nonsense," rejoined Burke, still standing, and with his very lips of an ashen paleness, "nonsense, Mike; what, in Heaven's name, brought you here?"

"Want, and a good will, sir. Money we must have, and will have."

"We! what's he doing here? George, I suppose you mean."

"Yes, George. We've been in London this six months, living, till I at least can live no longer, on what we can get. We must have money."

"Money! silence, Mike! Do you know that I could hang you?"

"Maybe; but two can play at that; I think I could hang you. You've most to lose, Mr. Burke; consider what I say. Five hundred pounds down and we leave the country."

"You have done so once, and here you are back again. Besides, George will not go."

"I think he will; he doesn't like the ould counthry; there's no play for poor men."

"Where is he?" said Burke, knitting his brow and his fingers pressing his under lip.

"In London. He came to see his mother who is sick. He was useful in Australia, and will never stop in England; the climate don't suit him. Besides, you owe us the money, Mr. Burke, and we want it."

"Want it indeed! so do many more; but what of Kildonald?"

"He's shot his last bolt, and lost; I don't think he can rise again."

"If he does, it's only to go down again. Have you seen the 'Hue and Cry?' You are not safe here for a day."

"Then give me the money; it's mine: and the paper has saved you."

"I tell you the paper was useless. Five hundred pounds! Where's it to come from?"

"We've nothing to do with that. We'll take care where it goes to. We'll be drinking your honour's health before the month's past." As Mike rose in spirits, Burke rose in temper. Burke was not constitutionally brave, but circumstances made him so; and it was clear to him that vacillation with a man like Mike was worse than useless, it was dangerous. Apparently while hesitating as to his answer, he tore one half of a sheet of paper, and going to the door, unlocked it.

"Phelim," said he, "get me a shilling stamp." In a few minutes he again opened the door, during which time Mike had again put on his disguise. His clerk presented him with the stamp.

"Now," said he, "this is a mere acknowledgment of a debt of 100l., for which I can sue you the moment you are known to be in this country; such a transaction need compromise neither of us. Sign your name to that. Nay! don't hesitate, Mike, for I can't afford to be robbed as often as you please for the eventual satisfaction of seeing you hanged."

"A hundred pounds!" laughed Mike; "nonsense, Misther Burke, the thing's impossible."

Burke took the key from the door and put it in his pocket. This was no place for a trial of strength, nor was Mike Heenan's position well fitted for the encounter. The relinquishment of 400l. gave him pain, but what was to be done? "I'll never do it." Burke stepped back to a

F 2

small and unobtrusive cabinet, well secured with
a lock, and opened it. When he turned round
again he held a pistol in his hand. Mike's
reliance had been in his moral strength; it
wouldn't do.

"You have said that you and I swim in the
same boat; I believe it, and I will not trust you.
Sign that paper, take your cheque, and never let
me see you here again."

Mike looked at the pistol. "What will George
say?"

"Never you mind what George will say. Sign
that paper; and when you set foot on Irish soil
again, it shall go into the hands of the tipstaff,
if needful. I would as soon be hanged in your
company as live in the atmosphere of the canting
hypocrites who surround us."

Mechanically then Mike Heenan signed it.
The pistol and the paper, with sundry other
valuable documents, were consigned to the strong
chest again (a movement not overlooked by the
astute client), and Mike was gone to divide his
spoil with the Egyptians.

Two nights afterwards an entrance was effected
into Burke's offices, and before the police arrived

they had been ransacked; the cabinet yielded
up its treasures, and, among other things, a
paper, by which it is doubtful how long Burke
will receive the Kildonald rents.

CHAPTER IV.

INDEPENDENCE.

" Miserum est alienæ incumbere famæ."—*Juv.*, viii. 761.

THERE is as much difference between the
advice a man gives himself and that which he
gets from his friends as there is between the
nauseous draught of the apothecary made up for
you and the dose of excellent port he reserves
for his own affectionate drinking. In the one
case you get a very palatable offering, the pre-
scription of a flatterer, which is not likely to be
of much service; in the other, the rough draught
of one who is likely to give you the best he has,
but not to make it too pleasant. One thing
makes me very chary of taking advice at all; it
is this: that no one can have the intimate acquaintance with your affairs which you possess
yourself; and without that intimacy his counsel
is likely to fall short of its true aim. Charlie
Thornhill was very much of this opinion. No-

body quite knew him—his brother least of all—
and nobody sympathized with him. His character was not one that courted confidence. He
was a great favourite with those men whom he
knew intimately, and his manly accomplishments
tended to make him acceptable with many more,
but there was scarcely one with whom he could
be identified as a close and intimate friend. It
might be a fault in his nature. He was shy,
and not clever; and he had a certain common
sense, and a feeling of right not so popular
amongst the young men of the world as it might
be. He had none of the sharpness which they
called common sense, and had an awkward
manner of calling things by their right names,
which made some men fight shy of him. But
most persons would have done him a favour, if
in their power; and the worst to be urged
against him was that he was not very amusing.
Almost every one admitted certain good qualities
of temper, courage, and honesty, but no one
thought of him as a person to be served. It is
true that appearances were against his standing
in need of it, and his natural reserve would have
effectually prevented his asking a favour, had he

seen his necessities as one or two persons saw them.

Lady Marston was not only a woman in all the best and kindest gifts of woman's nature— in its constancy and truth, in its affection and tenderness, in its forethought and tact, but in all the perseverance and active courage in behalf of her *protégés* which are supposed to belong to men and ministers in want of a return. She was not, therefore, likely to forget Charlie. She knew his necessities better than he did himself. She knew, too, how he could best help himself, for she had watched him from a boy. She knew his truth and his honest nature, his idleness and ignorance, and his strong good sense. But she knew how difficult it would be to help him in a world where everybody was fighting and struggling and cheating and bribing for self. Delicacy urged her to go to Mrs. Thornhill; but Mrs. Thornhill, since her husband's mysterious death, had been out of the world. She had no political influence, no politics. Then she thought of Tom, and she found him willing to support his brother, to give him half of his fortune, if he wanted it; in fact, to do anything but tease his friends for their interest with the Minister, or the Home Department, or the Foreign Office; for anything of which Charlie, to say truth, was not eminently fitted by his antecedents.

"But, my dear Lady Marston, what can he want with anything to do? He's welcome to anything I have, you know. There's always a home for him at Thornhills; lots of shooting— the best bird season I have known for years; and there's my black hack for him to ride. And when my uncle Henry dies, he'll have all that. And I only wish it was ten times as much for his sake."

"But you don't understand your brother's position, Tom. He ought to be independent of circumstances. Life's very uncertain; so is banking. Your uncle may live for forty years, or the bank may go to-morrow."

"Bless my soul! Lady Marston, how you frighten one! I hope it won't," said Tom Thornhill, laughing. "Let him come to Melton, and we'll put him up among us. You persuade him: he'll do anything for you."

Well, of course this was useless. It was no use wasting time on his brother; and Mary

Stanhope was not much better. "Charlie at business! Why, he'll be ill in a week. Besides, what's he to do? He'd better marry somebody. I suppose he will some day.. Why can't he go and live with his mother? that's the best place for a young man now-a-days. They're always in mischief."

From such sage advisers Lady Marston turned to Lord Tiverton. The Premier was a charming person, impervious to anything; always smiling or joking, *il se moquait de tout le monde*. He enjoyed the temperament of a duck's back. He was, however, a *beau garçon*, somewhat *passé*, and had a reputation for saying the pleasantest things in the world. A refusal was always a difficulty with him; to Lady Marston an impossibility.

"A favour, Lady Marston? A pleasure to grant it. Anything I can do. Of course we must manage something for him." And on he rattled. "Remember his father? Yes, poor fellow; indeed I do. Rather crotchety about the Game Laws for current opinion, but a capital fellow, capital fellow. Can he speak Spanish? because I think we could manage something. What? nothing but his own language? That's a bore. Now a little German or something of that sort goes a great way. Even if it's quite useless, and a man can neither speak it, read it, nor write it, still in these days, you know, public opinion must be considered. Perhaps he could *say* he knew something about it, and take his chance. He *might* satisfy the examiners. It's all great nonsense. I'm sure I couldn't pass an examination myself. Yes, yes, we must do something for him. Why doesn't his brother go into Parliament ? "

It was very vague, and Lady Marston knew the world too well to place much reliance upon it, so she turned her fascinations next upon Lord Thomas Charter. Little Tommy Charter, or little Lord Tommy, as he was familiarly called by the great unwashed, was brother of a Whig duke, the first statesman in England, the most popular of reformers, author of " The Life of Mumbo Jumbo," the African traveller, and " The History of his own Times," and everybody else's. He was a small, sallow, sharp-featured man, highly conscientious, and who stuck to his party through thick and thin, whichever it happened to be.

"Busy, Lady Marston? Indeed I am. But, never mind; let us see what can be done. I suppose we are sure of Marston on the Episcopal Clearance Bill? the country gets more practical every day. There's the Sand and Blotting-paper Office: can't we do something for your friend in that? Examination? True, true; but it's very trifling. History of England—good knowledge of modern Europe, in fact, very essential—Italy especially; she's in a very peculiar position: couple of modern languages; say French and German: Latin absolutely necessary—a little of it; but no earthly use: a science or two; and mathematics, of course. By-the-way, tell your friend to be well up in the provisions of the Great Charter. No man ever yet did any good in this world who didn't appreciate the efforts of Stephen Langton and his followers."

Lady Marston was not sanguine enough to imagine that Charlie Thornhill would qualify (as he would have called it) for this stake; but she could not but thank the great statesman for his kindness, and say that she hoped she should be able to write to him a line in a day or two. Lord Tommy knew nothing of sinecures; his whole life had been spent in abolishing jobs and distributing patronage according to merit—or at least professing to do so, when everybody was looking on. He was the very man who had lately discarded his third wife's half-brother, a young man from the Board of Bricks and Mortar, enjoying his 800*l.* per annum, for irregularity. At the end of the first month he was reported, at the end of the second reprimanded, at the end of the third he was reported again, and by the end of the fourth he was dismissed, and another reigned in his stead. It is true that he had married somewhat discreditably upon the 800*l.* per annum, and it was necessary to make an example to deter others from following so bad an example. Strange fatality! his name, too, was Charles. The Charlies were an unlucky lot.

The next person to whom Lady Marston applied was the late Wentworth Jones, now Lord Silkstone. At Eton he was Bill Jones, rather a swell, high up in the sixth, and a very good fellow. At Christchurch he became Wentworth Jones, forgetting the Billy, and report said pretty truly that he had come into a good fortune

as well as a good name.   Then he went into
Parliament, worked hard, had a ready wit, and
unfailing memory for other persons' shortcom-
ings, which made him an invaluable debater;
for though deficient in knowledge he was never
afraid to display his ignorance.   Such valuable
qualities could not be overlooked: he was taken
by the hand by the Premier, and by the nose
by Lord Tommy, who found him very useful
for a time, and when he was in the way had
him elevated to the peerage under the title of
Baron Silkstone.   From that day the little
Joneses became Honourable Wentworths, and
their father became more polished, more civil,
and less sincere than ever.   He rode the neatest
of hacks, had the smallest of grooms, wore the
best-cut coats, and the most lemon-coloured
gloves of any man in England.

When he was first applied to on behalf of
our hero he suggested at once the colonies.
He was overpowered by his wish to serve so
charming a person as Lady Marston.   How he
longed for whole hosts of governorships of South
Pacific Islands, secretaryships of Pulo Penangs,
commissionerships of Jungleguava, attachéships

to the embassy of Owhyee, and half a dozen other ships of every line but the right one! And now, when pressed to say what he could positively hold out, he made a definite promise of a nice snug little sinecure on the coast of Western Africa, within easy reach of M. du Chaillu's cannibals, and where Charlie would succeed a gentleman who had been eaten alive by a crocodile whilst performing his ablutions. The charming smile, white teeth, and bland *empressement* with which it was offered enhanced the value of this desirable post, and it was with considerable difficulty that Lady Marston could refuse it in sufficiently polite terms.

"I am really exceedingly obliged, Lord Silkstone, for the interest you so kindly take in my friend Mr. Thornhill, but the young man for whom I am asking the favour is strong and healthy at present, and might, if taken in his raw state, disagree with the crocodiles."

I've never heard that the Honourable Wentworth was selected to fill the post vacated by the hardy bather.

Having waited a short time for something to turn up, and not hearing from either of her ministerial friends of anything more promising than the West African Station, Lady Marston consulted her husband.

Sir Frederick Marston was a sensible, accomplished man; practical in all points; fond of the world in which he lived, in no bad sense; very modern in his ideas, though not without a hopeful touch of chivalry in his nature. He married his wife because he loved her, but he was not the less happy to find that she adorned her station, and was exactly fitted to be " Lady Marston." The consequence of his appreciation was a happy mixture of deference and affection, and that sort of intercourse which results from a mutual conviction of each other's capabilities.

" Well! Frederick, nothing has been done for Charles Thornhill yet."

" My dear, you seem to look upon Charles in the light of a pauper."

" So he is, to all intents and purposes. I can hardly conceive a more painful position than that of a man able and willing to work, but compelled to live upon the charity of others."

" Surely a mother's offering to a son's necessities is scarcely charity ? "

"Up to a certain age, no; afterwards, yes. And what charms me with Charlie is, that he feels it to be so."

"It's the case with half the aristocracy, where no provision can be, or has been, made for the younger children. What's the use of a large house and a comfortable jointure?"

"Mrs. Thornhill has not too large a jointure, Frederick; and, though she can well afford a home and a few hundreds for a younger son, Charlie's view of his own position is the true one. So let us help him as far as we can."

"With all my heart, my dear; but that won't make him independent. There's very little real independence in this world; and if there were much, what a terrible set of savages we should be! The only really independent person of my acquaintance is my trainer, Turner; and he not only does as he likes with his own, but with mine too."

"Well, then, independent or not, will you help him to do as he likes?" said Lady Marston, checking her husband's inclination for a discussion, of which Sir Frederick was remarkably fond.

"Will a Government office suit him?" asked the baronet.

"I think not, if it means an examination without some preparation. And if he has that, he may as well go into the army, which he has talked of a hundred times."

"Well, an examination of some sort he must have: not very severe, I apprehend. Whether it does much good, I don't know. I think we shall have an inferior class of men, well prepared for special service, but not likely to make such good general servants. The education of a gentleman usually fits a man for any duties we have to put him to."

"Excepting in modern languages," said Lady Marston.

"No English boys can know much about them, unless educated abroad. And a comparison with us and foreigners in this respect is unfair: the Continent throws men of all languages together: there is both a greater facility for acquiring them, and a readier means for exercising them. But I don't think we're much behind them in essentials—eh, Kate? And you know I was a terrible reformer in that line once upon a time.

No; Charlie will do best for a grenadier, or the household brigade."

" I almost agree with you ; and if he reads for the one he will fit himself for anything that may fall out by the way. And now the sooner he is out of London the better. We must find a good tutor for him, who'll read with him and teach him to read for himself. That's rather out of my line, Frederick," said Lady Marston, who was beginning to think she had entered upon a rather too masculine undertaking. " However, you and he can settle that between you. Only, if you have anything to do with it, beware of Gilsland, and don't let him get too near Melton." With this sage advice Lady Marston started on some other benevolent errand, and Sir Frederick went into committee on the Buffertown railway, and forgot, for a time, the very existence of his wife's *protégé*.

Charlie, the person most concerned in these arrangements, was in the mean time enjoying himself as we have seen; but he was constantly visited with an anxious desire to do something for himself. He knew he was leading an unprofitable sort of existence, and envied hundreds

who would like to have changed places with him:
that's natural. Charlie had not much light, as
the Reverend Struggle Muffins would say; but
what he had was pretty clear. He did not get
into mischief with his eyes shut; and, though
that is the more excusable error, it is not the
less dangerous. Hitherto he might have been
described as some horses—he always had a leg
to spare. He passed his time very comfortably;
but the thought was constantly recurring that
he ought to be doing something else. I do not
think that it ever occurred to Charlie Thornhill
that the whole of the set were going down hill,
or that there was something abstractedly wrong
in wasting time, gambling, getting in debt, and
the like. He had not been educated in a strict
school of discipline. He thought it wrong for
himself, because he individually could not afford
it. Time was wanted to strengthen the growth
of principles which seemed almost inherent in
his nature, if such things be. He seems to have
been honest by nature, thoughtful by nature,
courageous by nature, chivalrous by nature: as
yet he had tried to improve none of nature's
gifts. He had a speedy way of administering

rough justice of his own; he liked good eating and drinking; was an active enemy to poaching, vulpecide, and dissent, and had a horror of books; these were the gifts of education. When he wanted a cheque he went to his mother; when he wanted advice or sympathy, to Lady Marston; when he wanted what he knew to be decidedly wrong, and what would be met by remonstrance from either of these, he went to Mary Stanhope.

He had a great deal of conversation with Sir Frederick; as much, in fact, as that legislator could find time for. He held out no great prospects in a Government official situation; besides which, the thing was in itself distasteful to Charlie. As the matter of consultation was only a compliment to his former guardian, he was not long in coming to a decision in favour of pipeclay; and it then only remained to look for a tutor.

Tutors are of various kinds. There is the well-educated University man, rather stiff, formal, whose ex-parochial existence is passed amongst dry tomes; who reads strictly with his natural enemies for a certain number of hours each day,

addresses them as Mr., greets them night and
morning with a bland smile and courtly bow,
imparts what he knows, which is not much of
modern requirements, and is not eminently successful in his calling.

There is the rough-and-ready, pipe-smoking,
slovenly tutor; a clever, well-informed, half-idle,
half-energetic person, of seedy coat and unkempt
hair. Cares little enough about any tastes, in-
clinations, or habits for good or evil, but goes
the shortest possible road to a certain object, by
cramming and coaching, and talking and repeat-
ing, until he thinks the head is full which came
to be filled. How soon it empties itself again is
another question, but is not in the bond.

There is your respectable country clergyman,
whose only qualifications are his former scholar-
ship and his present necessities. Little enough
is done in such hands, except (if he is fortunate
enough to have a daughter or two, which all of
them have) love-making. An excellent man is
he, and as unfit to restrain impetuous youth, to
deal with idleness and deceit, to direct a mis-
guided mind, or urge a slothful one, as any man
alive. He would teach, if his pupils would

learn; but he has neither persuasion nor vigour to induce them to do so.

Above all, there is your utter incapable—not impossibly an old soldier; who, having dissipated time and money on whist and sangaree, comes home to discover that there is one profession still open to a gentleman. Knowing nothing, he sets to work to teach it. Finding that even impossible, he sends for assistance. Lo! there appears a third-rate Cambridge man, whom a career of low dissipation had almost stranded, when his happy chance—*the education of youth*—presents itself. Perhaps an Irishman, a Dublin B.A., a capital mathematician when sober, willing to teach anything from hopscotch to the binomial theorem, takes a part in the guidance of the pupil. Then a Frenchman or German hair-dresser, who is always a political refugee, not unfrequently in correspondence with exiled royalty, is engaged to teach modern language. A drawing-master does his department, and a lecturer from the Polytechnic does the natural sciences, unless that falls also to the share of the versatile Irishman. As to the chief, he disdains work, an does no department whatever.

But we waste time. It was to one of the latter that Charlie was introduced before long, who, to his natural urbanity, added a vicinity to Gilsland: the latter point carried the day. Charlie went to bed in the consciousness of having done something for himself, and Captain Armstrong retired to rest happy in having added one more to the list of his victims.

CHAPTER V.

TWO OF A TRADE.

" Have more than thou showest ;
Speak less than thou knowest."—*Lear*, i. 4.

To a dingy-looking house of considerable size, in one of the numerous streets which run parallel to Portland Place—be it Wimpole Street, Harley Street, or any other, matters not—I beg to transport my reader. There is a heavy respectability in the sombre darkness which belongs to this quarter. The carriages, "rari in gurgite nantes," are of the heavy order; round, sleek, fat, pursy horses; family coachmen; yellow chariots, or long and low barouches, stand about at 4 P.M. at intervals. Paralytic old ladies, with wondrous bonnets of flowers, feathers, or bugles, and shaking ringlets, the undeniable handiwork of Mr. Truefitt, come creeping out on the arms of their footmen, and here and there a pretty girl, with airs tottering on the steps of Belgravian

audacity, rustles down the doorsteps in attendance on dear grandmamma. Here is the house
of a millionnaire merchant, who disdains the
fashionable *quartier*, and sticks to his prejudices.
Magnificent collections of water-colours adorn
the walls; articles of vertu cover the ormolu and
mosaic tables; costly wines, port unknown in
regal cellars, and choice Madeira of many a
voyage, stock the cellar; and a not inglorious
hospitality is shared with men of his own time
and weight, which is never under sixteen stone,
and may be four - and - twenty. There is the
abode of a prosperous banker; a junior in one
of the great City firms—a junior only; for your
chief of the firm affects Piccadilly and the *beau
monde*, has a stud in Gorsehamptonshire, and a
moor in Scotland, and entertains his West-end
clients. But the junior is rich and old, and will
be richer, if older. For he loves nothing but
himself and his money, and is alone in the world.
He has quarrelled with his only sister years ago,
for disgracing herself and him by marrying a
handsome Irish scapegrace (at that time about
town, but having since disappeared under conviction of "nobbling," and some suspicions of

manslaughter), called Kildonald. He has heard of her since, in childbirth in a foreign country, in sickness, and in want, but he has never relented towards her and the innocent children for whom she pleaded. He is nearly twenty years her senior, and once loved Norah, and took care of her. But she left his house, and he cannot forget it; he is proud to think that his prophecies of Kildonald have been more than fulfilled. He knew him better than she. Such is Roger Palmer; of the firm of Mint, Chalkstone, Palmer, and Co., Bankers, of East Goldbury, City, London.

Roger Palmer had treated himself to a little fire; the evenings, he remarked to himself, get cold in October, and others remarked to themselves that Roger Palmer was getting older every day. He had eaten a good dinner, and was not so much out of temper as he looked. He was white, small, fragile, with pinched features and a very fair complexion. His mouth was very thin-lipped and close, and his forehead was low, but broad. He did not want intellect, but was wholly without high aspirations. He loved money for itself, and his cold, silent, badly-furnished rooms testified it. He was a childless widower, and he did not lament the loss of his wife so much as he rejoiced in the curtailment of his expenses. As a young man he was not penurious, only careful. He loved to have a large balance, in case of emergencies: as he grew richer the feeling strengthened, and now he was a simple miser. Money was his god; he hugged it and worshipped it, as God is seldom worshipped; but he would not burn it, as an idol, to keep himself warm. Well! there he sat, over his little fire, warming himself and his bright old toes; for he was scrupulously clean, and could not forget that he was of the firm of Mint, Chalkstone, and Co. And by degrees odd matters assumed a form. The old man saw his sister, as she was when he first took her to a small house in London, before he became a partner in the bank. Then he wondered whether her children had inherited her grace and beauty, and her self-will—this last thought was a little compromise. Then he thought of Kildonald, his good-looking face, his bad reputation, his grace of manner, his latitude of principle, his turf practices, and his final disappearance. " Thornhill! Ah! poor Thornhill!"

thought he; "but for his kindness what should I have been? Where would have been Mint, who never saw a race, and Chalkstone, who never played a rubber, and the Co.? We must all have gone in the panic, but for the propping and bolstering of Henry Thornhill and his kind-hearted brother Geoffrey."

Two or three weeks after this soliloquy, Roger Palmer found himself in the little parlour at the back of the banking-house in Pall Mall, face to face with Henry Thornhill. Never were men less alike, physically and mentally. The one was robust, fresh-looking, handsome; the other, mean-looking and business-like, with an air of sharpness out of place west of Temple Bar. The one was kindly and well-mannered, and abrupt in spite of his nature; the other was husky and dry, and only genial upon principle. There in his leathern chair sat the West-end banker, and over against him the City man of business. Both had a respect for certain qualities of the other: one was exalted by absolute superiority, the other assumed temporal equality by a great act of studied and unusual justice, which he was there to do. After a few minutes' conversation, there-

fore, and leaning forward with his elbows upon
the arms of the chair he occupied, Roger
Palmer said, " Thornhill, you know what we
owe you, you, who are occupied in the same
pursuits, who have the same anxieties; and I
look upon it as an obligation that can never be
repaid."

" Well, Palmer, be it so," replied the other;
" it is long ago, and I think you would have
done the same by us. You attach too much
credit to my personal share of the business. I
am only glad that by means of poor Geoffrey
I was able to help you."

" Help! God help you in a like case, my
friend!" said the little miser cordially, and
almost wringing his hands with the recollection.
" It was life to us; we were gone—at our last
gasp—Thornhills saved us. Oh, how often I've
thought of that Sunday night, which seemed to
separate us from ruin and disgrace! But I want
another favour, Thornhill."

" There's no Geoffrey now, Palmer. What is
it? surely not money?"

" Yes, money, money; but a surplus. I want
your advice. Will you be my executor?   I

must make my will; that's the load on my mind at present."

"What's become of your sister, Roger Palmer? you had one once. Where is she? what is she doing?" asked Henry Thornhill.

"No, no, hush! I've sworn, never—not one stiver;" and the old man frowned, and his lips closed so tightly as to disappear, whilst thick veins swelled in his forehead. "She laughed me to scorn; she eat of my bread and drank of my cup, and when the wolf came she turned to him in spite of the shepherd's warning. I might be generous, but now I mean to be just."

"Then be just and generous at the same time, and leave your money to your own relatives," said the West-end tradesman.

"It's what you will do, I presume," rejoined the City magnate; "but you know nothing of the ingratitude of women, as I do."

"Of course not;" and a deep sigh was following, which Henry Thornhill suppressed with a strong effort; "of course not. But if you do not leave your money, as I tell you, to Mrs. Kildonald or her children, I'll have nothing to do with it. There, Palmer, we're old friends

and need not quarrel ; but you know my
mind."

Henry Thornhill was too generous to add the
repayment of an obligation to his advocacy of
what was right. But Roger Palmer had done
what we all do occasionally for ourselves : he
had fashioned a course of justice in accordance
with his own inclination, and intended to abide
by it.

"And your nephews, your brother's boys, how
are they ? what are they doing ? "

"The elder is spending money, like his poor
father ; and the younger—well, the younger is
thinking of making it, if he can ; that's like you,
you know." And Henry Thornhill smiled a
grim smile as he clutched his friend's extended
hand.

"Does he need it ? does he want a profession ? " said the little man, eagerly.

"As much as any one that wishes to be
independent, and is not so."

"Then why not take him in here ? What an
opening for him ! "

"Humph ! that's as may be. Perhaps he
might be better with you," said the uncle.

" Oh, come, come, Thornhill, nonsense! Now think of what I've said. Bless my heart, it's a provision for the Prince of Wales."

"And you think of what I've said; and do as you ought to do with your money. When you've made up your mind to follow my advice, come to me, and I'll be your executor. Good-by." And Roger Palmer departed on his way eastward, and Henry Thornhill sat down again to a ledger, but his thoughts were far away from the back parlour in Pall Mall.

It will be seen that there subsisted a considerable intimacy between these two men, so different. Circumstances had thrown them together, and an obligation due, with a generous mind, knits the debtor more firmly to the creditor. Thornhill knew all he had done for Palmer; and with all his penurious hardness the latter had never been unmindful of it. In fact, he went to Pall Mall that day with the intention of leaving his money to a Thornhill. He had ascertained sufficient for his purpose; and although he was prevented from announcing that purpose to Henry Thornhill, he had quite determined in his own mind that Charlie would be none the worse for his patronage and assistance. He liked what he had seen of him, and he had no particular wish that his wealth should go to replace an estate which was being, according to all accounts, rapidly dissipated. How little he knew of the use to which his money might some day be put the reader shall know hereafter, if his patience will carry him through the task he has commenced.

In the meantime, our hero has carried out his intention honestly enough. Charlie was reading hard. He was involved in the intricacies of that erudite and interesting history called "Chepmell," from which he ascertained the names of the heptarchy, the difference between Pitt and Lord Chatham, and the descent of our reigning monarch from James I. of glorious memory. Euclid had already informed him that the square of the hypotenuse was equal to the squares of the other two sides of a right-angled triangle; but whether he was to add that it was "absurd" or not, he was not yet certain. He was making daily translations from M. Contanseau's extracts from Charles XII.—the battle of Pultava and his doings among the Janissaries—

as very likely to be set; and he had almost con-
quered the difficulty of "quantitative and quali-
tative" adjectives, and the meaning of a thing
called "the objective case," from a modern
Lindley Murray. The assistance he derived in
all this from *Old* Armstrong, as that gallant
captain was called, was but small: such as the
unhappy victim of short whist who never held a
trump and played execrably, and nocturnal
jorums of hot gin-and-water, might be expected
to furnish. The Armstrong table was more substantial than *recherché*, and the ladies of the
family were a moderate substitute for the plea-
santries of Marston House, Lady Elizabeth, Mrs.
Thornhill, and Mary Stanhope, or the charms
of Edith Dacre and her sister. Mrs. Armstrong
was a slatternly beauty of forty-five; Miss Armstrong was a pretty girl, adorned in many colours,
who found everything "awfully jolly" or "hard
lines," who sang manly songs, with a dash of the
comic, made her own bonnets, painted scrolls for
the curate of the parish, and was evidently
destined for the first eligible spoon who was lucky
enough to get an ensigncy through her father's
agency. The Cambridge man was a terrible dis-

appointment. He had no knowledge of Newmarket, nor of the Fitzwilliam. He preferred
beer and cavendish to regalias and sherry and
soda-water; and asked with considerable *naïveté*
what Mr. Thornhill wanted with that huge can
of cold water every morning? Charlie, however,
had a strong will, and for some weeks made considerable progress in spite of all difficulties. He
had his pleasures, too. Mary Stanhope's kindness had touched him nearly. He laughed at
her fears for his health, but he accepted his
favourite horse, and showed his appreciation of
her liberality by riding him straight and well
whenever he was fit to go. He had stuck to his
first refusal to join his brother at Melton; but
he treated resolution by a dinner and bed now
and then at Gilsland, and he was not always back
so early the next day as he promised himself.
He set a capital example, not unaccompanied by
precept, to his fellow-pupils, who held him in
some respect, not only for his years, but for some
preconceived notions of his *savoir vivre.* " Why
the deuce don't you fellows read?" said he.
" Old Armstrong swears you'll none of you get
through the exam."

" He knows nothing about it; I don't believe
he can construe this bit of Livy himself," said
Craven, who had come from Eton, where, he
admitted, that he had never opened a book or
done a verse yet. Smith's time had been passed
at the village public, making love to the Hebe
of the tap-room, until Charlie Thornhill had
laughed at his not very delicate amour, and made
him understand that a roadside public was not
quite the place for an old Harrovian. Marlborough and Cheltenham furnished each their
quota; and the language of the representatives of
these seminaries of polite learning had to be
corrected by some very unmistakeable hints from
a gentleman not squeamish, I regret to say, as to
an occasional oath, but with a just discrimination
between what was wrong and what was low.

" What made you fellows tell such a falsehood
to Armstrong about having been on the river
to-day?" said Charlie. " You know you hadn't
been near a boat." Charlie hated a lie, and
seldom failed to show it.

" Oh, what *does* it signify? He's an old fool,
and never knows anything about it," said one;
whilst another hung his head, and said, " Why

shouldn't one say the river as well as anything else ? "

" Because," said Charlie, " though he's not very bright, he always treats us like gentlemen, and it's not pleasant to sit by and hear it."

" Well, it wasn't the right thing to do," said Smith.

" No, hanged if it was !" said Craven. " Let's tell him to-morrow we were over at Saddington, playing billiards. Hallo! there he goes, to a muffin-struggle with the Dragon " (this was Mrs. Armstrong) ; " he's going to have a rubber with the Doctor ; let's have a lark. I shall do my work to-morrow. Cantabs will give us a coach, so I shall go and smoke a pipe."

This is a sample of the state of things under the laxed discipline of the gallant captain, late of the H.E.I.C. There is, however, no doubt that he had much for which to thank Charlie Thorn-hill, who neither smoked pipes under his nose, laughed at his wife, chaffed his daughter, fre-quented the pot-house, cut prayers, or bullied him in any way. Before the winter he had worked a reformation which was manifest to so dense an intellect as the Captain's ; and Charlie

was happy in believing that he knew something
more than he did when he left Gresham's. He
was a mark for the arrows of the young women
of the neighbourhood, which caused him a little
trouble at first, as he hated letter-writing and
was not quite safe in his spelling. Miss Pil-
borough, the doctor's daughter, asked him to tea,
on pink paper, and in the name of her mother.
The rector, old Cureton, went the length of a
dinner; and a neighbouring squireen, who had
heard of his brother and remembered his father's
death, left his own card and his wife's, with Mr.
Thornhill's name in the corner, and an inti-
mation that there was breakfast and the hounds
at Topham Scrubs on the following Monday.
Charlie's horse was not fit, and Edith Dacre
reigned supreme.

CHAPTER VI.

A CATASTROPHE.

"Prepare him early with instruction, and season his mind
with the maxims of truth."

"AND who was the wife of Charles I., Mr.
Thornhill?" said Captain Armstrong, as he sat
with his book before him, superintending a sort
of morning canter in English history.

"Edith Dacre," said Charlie. "Oh, no! I
beg your pardon, Captain Armstrong. I mean—
let me see—'pon my soul, I forget; but I was
thinking of something else. How very stupid, to
be sure!"

"'Charles was also engaged to Henrietta
Maria, sister of Louis XIII.,'" said the Captain
very gravely, reading from the book. "'Just
before this marriage took place James I. died,
March, 1625.'"

"Of course—of course; I beg your pardon."
And the lecture proceeded with no very satis-

factory result, as far as Charlie was concerned. A reference to the book showed the Capain that his pupil was wrong upon two or three points, of which he himself was not quite safe, as " that the area of a triangle was double its altitude with its base," and that " Edward II.'s widow was confined for life to the Castle of Gilsland." If the reader requires any explanation of an ignorance which is not uncommon either in teacher or pupil, he will find it in this case in the following note, which was at the very moment in our hero's left-hand waistcoat pocket. It had arrived that morning by post. It produced a greater sensation than the contents appear to warrant :—

GILSLAND, Tuesday Morning.

"DEAR MR. THORNHILL,

"Mamma desires me to write, as she is much engaged, and ask whether you will give us the pleasure of your company from Friday till Monday next. The hounds meet at our cover on Saturday, and perhaps you can send your horse over on Friday morning. There is a stall at your service. My brother is here, as he is

not yet gone to Berne. We hope you will be
able to come.

"Yours very truly,

"EDITH DACRE."

Charlie had dined before at Gilsland, and slept
there. He had been out hunting in his life often
enough to have borne the news of the meet with
equanimity: and Mr. Dacre's cover, though a
sure find, was a very moderate one for sport.
The fact is that this was the first time he had
ever had a letter from Edith; and, though difficult to extract much from it, in the way of great
encouragement, he managed to pick out of it
consolation enough to drive out all the effects
of his previous day's reading. Finding himself
unfit for serious work, he lit a cigar, and visited
the stable. The Templar was fit, and his proper
day was Thursday. It was early in the season;
there was no sign of frost in the air, he counter-
manded the Thursday's meet, and ordered his
horse to be sent on Friday in good time to Gilsland. So much for the effects of a little scented
paper, and an invitation to dinner; and he gave
up Stickborough gorse almost without a sigh.

"If Mrs. Armstrong and the Captain will excuse me," said Charlie, at breakfast (and the Dragon was never so politely addressed by any one else in the house), " I shall be away from to-day till Monday."

"We shall be very sorry to lose you, I'm sure, Mr. Thornhill," said she, with considerable *empressement*, and smirking at Matilda; "very sorry. I wonder where it is that Mr. Thornhill hides himself occasionally from Saturday till Monday?" An intelligent titter between the ladies, and a plodding stoical indifference to everything but the dinner on the part of the gentlemen. Charlie, however, felt no bashfulness, as he answered—

" Gilsland, Mrs. Armstrong ; it's about eighteen miles from here."

" Gilsland—Gilsland—let me see," said the Captain, rushing at once into the subject, and very much fuddled with a morning potation. "Why, that's where Edward I.—no, II., was confined—no, it was his wife. We had it in our lecture the day before yesterday."

" Captain Armstrong," said the Dragon, quite shocked, " do you know what you're talking about?

—Matilda, my dear." And the lady left the room.

There was a goodly party assembled at the Dacres' on Friday, at seven P.M. : a heavy divine; two fox-hunting squires, and their wives; a foreign nobleman, who had a house in the neighbourhood for the winter; a dowager peeress; Mr. and Lady Elizabeth Montague Mastodon; Mr. Robinson Brown, junior; Mr. De Beauvoir, and Charlie Thornhill. A very meritorious impression has gone abroad that horse-flesh is *never* a subject of conversation before the claret appears. Our old acquaintance Nimrod assures us that at Melton, after that brilliant run which was honoured with a niche in the " Quarterly," the subject of hunting was not once mentioned during dinner. This is a simple misconception of the rules of good society, where people usually talk, as they eat and drink, of the things that please them best. Beer was not excluded from the table at Gilsland, nor was hunting a proscribed guest. The divine had his say on the subject of tithe commutation and the church-rate, into the former of which Mr. Mastodon introduced the hop-duty, and into the latter an educational scheme of his own. The dowager peeress started Paris, in pity to the foreigner, who was not well-up in English politics, and which all joined in hustling about till they got to the fashions. Here the squires pulled up, and their wives took up the running. Charlie had not said much, for, having got next to Edith, and opposite to Alice, he satisfied himself with thinking. Edith never talked quite so much to Charlie as to other people; and Robinson Brown ran away with the conversation on the other side of her completely. Alice and De Beauvoir were discussing the charms of a certain picture by Millais; in which the gentleman fondly insinuated a certain resemblance to the principal figure, but which Miss Dacre as strongly repudiated, with very good reason.

"That's no compliment, Mr. De Beauvoir; the woman looks as if she had been pressed in a mangle, and then ironed to get out the creases; and I hope you don't consider my hair bright red!"

And she turned and looked at her admirer with a frank and open gaze, that assured Charlie, if he ever had any fears for Tom's chance against that gentleman. For he had lately discovered that Tuftenham, like all other male gossips, always arrived at some wrong conclusion; and that it was Alice, and not Edith, who was the "pretty sister" whom De Beauvoir affected, and not the young lady about whom he had so inconsiderately made himself uncomfortable. De Beauvoir had risen in his estimation since the discovery, and Robinson Brown was the person of whom, with much justice, he always spoke as "that ass." That ass was basking in sunshine at the present moment, and not grazing by any means on thistles. He drank, too, as they are said to do, of the sweetest water, and was well-nigh intoxicating himself. For Edith Dacre had a charming manner—so lively, so free, so unconsciously coquettish and unaffected, that a wiser man than Mr. Robinson Brown might have calculated on conquest. If Charlie had known the world as well as he afterwards learnt it, he might have considered it a good sign that he was an exception to this rule; that she lost her lightness, and assumed a gravity which she was catching unconsciously from him. "Dear Jane," however, was the greatest fool alive, and no wonder it was taken in.

"Iron," said Lady Elizabeth, who had too much sense ever to be above the shop, "demand for iron, of course there must be; as traffic increases, and population in large towns becomes denser, and gold flows in from these newly-found regions of which we hear so much, of course they'll want iron. We shall have an iron age again, Mr. Sylvester."

"And a golden one," said the gentleman, who seldom perpetrated a *bon mot;* "no more war— nothing but peace and plenty; that's a little against iron, my Lady."

"Peace! bless my heart! there'll be more war than ever. When people grow fast and rich, they kick, and then others kick again. Poor people go to war, sir? Oh, no. Where's the money to come from? Nobody goes to war without metal, you know."

And here Sylvester looked so puzzled at Mr. Dacre's "Bravo! Lady Elizabeth!" that, had he not been relieved by Sir Thomas Fallowtop, I can't say how long she would have been without a reply. The baronet, however, had a grievance. Iron had entered into his soul, and now was the time to relieve himself.

"I know that the consumption of metal must be much greater than formerly," said the plethoric baronet, with much dignity, "though I presume it has not become dearer through the increased demand; for the farmers all round our country have taken to use it for fencing, and it's a most dangerous obstacle to crossing a country. Something must be done by the legislature. You ruin this country as soon as you put an end to fox-hunting." The old gentleman looked for a seconder.

"Of course—most undoubtedly—vewy, vewy true," said Robinson Brown. "Tewwible thing indeed; awistocwacy's pleasures, and that sort of thing, eh, Miss Dacre?"

"I hope, Sir Thomas, that we shan't go into your country to-morrow then, for I am going out with the hounds. I've often been promised, and at last I am really going on horseback. I'm going to jump, too—ain't I, Teddy?"

"The mare's a capital fencer," said Teddy Dacre, "but she's rather troublesome to ride.

Edith has some peculiar opinions about gentlemen's hands, and she has insisted upon showing
us how to ride to-morrow. Mind your neck,
Charlie!"

Charlie thought of somebody else's neck, and
only said—

"I don't think you ought to let your sister
ride that mare, unless she's quieter than when I
saw her."

" Oh, how provoking you are, Mr. Thornhill!
Mamma and papa set such value on my neck
and your opinion about horses, that if you say
much more I sha'n't go at all."

Charlie held his tongue, which he found easier
than talking; but he made up his mind to
ascertain all about the mare, and act accordingly. He thought Alice might help him in the
drawing-room.

An hour later, Mr. Dacre shook the hand of
his last retiring guest, adding, " Good night!
We shall draw our covers first, and if we get a
run, well and good; if not, our second find will
be Fallowtops, notwithstanding the iron fences,
which have half-spoilt the riding, and ought to
be put a stop to by the landlords; they are the

only people to do it, and not by abuse, but remonstrance."

On a return to the drawing-room, the riding expedition of the next day was the topic of general conversation. The general feeling was against the qualifications of the mare for carrying a lady; but Teddy Dacre laughed at the notion, and Edith declared she could ride her, had ridden her, and would ride her; and Edith was a bit of a tyrant, and her word, on her own business, had long been law. Mr. Robinson Brown offered a substitute, and proposed to take the mare himself; but Miss Edith declared that his mother and sisters would never forgive her, if anything happened to him, and he had better reserve himself for his match with Mr. Thornhill. "Dear Jane" was accustomed to be treated with deference at home, and did not understand young ladies' chaff. Charlie had nothing to offer, as his own horse was quite unfit for any lady to ride.

"Oh! I should not care about you, you know, Mr. Thornhill; but the fact is, that I mean to ride the mare. Papa means to go with us on a hack, and I dare say you'll be good-natured enough to keep an eye upon us." Charlie went up to blood-heat, Fahrenheit. " Mamma would feel better satisfied." He was down at 32°. Before bedtime, however, Alice had made him a participator, to a certain extent, in her own fears.

" The mare is very hot with hounds," said she, " and, though Edith rides very well, she has a great deal more courage than experience."

" Then I won't be far away," said he, and the ladies went to bed.

There have been such things as hunt breakfasts described before this. I believe I know all about the breeches and boots, the neckerchiefs, and the cut of the pink, which has descended from the dignity of the old-fashioned swallow-tail through gradations of wide-skirted riding-coats, frock-coats, and shooting-jackets, to the present comfortably-fitting and truly useful morning coat, thick, warm, strong, and easy. But no sooner do I get among the pork-pie hats and the flyaway turbans, the pheasant breasts and partridge wings, the pilot spencers and velvet bodies, the short habits and curious nether garments of the Amazon of 1862, than I lose myself altogether, and become a miserable peg for envious critics to hang their gibes upon. Suffice it to say that Charlie appeared the perfection of an English sportsman, having assumed for the time a coat of modest black, as the garb best fitted for his present *status pupillaris ;* and Edith took her seat in a very proper habit befitting her intentions, and that chimney-pot which, with all the vagaries of modern taste, continues to be the head-dress of the most correct portion of our female equestrians.

By eleven o'clock the hounds, and servants with their masters' horses; a score of second horsemen; farmers of every grade, shape, age, and character ; two hard-riding doctors (they always are so); a first-flight parson ; and about fifty county gentlemen, who had partaken, or declined to partake, of Mr. Dacre's morning hospitality, were assembled in the field on the other side of the sunk fence.   Opposite the door of the house, grooms were leading the horses of those who prolonged their morning meal.   There was Mr. Dacre's favourite hack, a neat-looking animal enough, fit to carry a thin gentlemanly old man such as he.   There was Robinson Brown's three-hundred-guinea Irish Birdcatcher horse, all that size and length, length of tooth included, could make him. Even now Edith ought to have changed her mind and the groom the saddles. There was a good, useful, not very expensive hunter for Teddy Dacre himself, and the mare, which switched her narrow, blood-like quarters and clean-made thighs and hocks with her tail, now and then putting back her ears and striking with one leg; and there was Charlie's young one, Mary Stanhope's present—Aunt Mary, who was determined to make him idle, if possible—a raw, lengthy, slack-looking horse, but with large limbs, good shoulders, and great depth. His fault lay behind the saddle; but there was time as well as room for improvement there.

"Where to, Dacre?" said the Master, throwing himself into his saddle, and giving at the same time an order to his huntsman.

"Yes, sir," replied that functionary, touching his cap, "there's a fox lies down by the osiers, close against the river." And away went the huntsman in the midst of his hounds, preceded by one whip and followed by another, towards the supposed fox-kennel.

After drawing two or three spinneys on the road, blank, giving an opportunity to Charlie to superintend his charge, whose mare fidgeted about considerably, and had relieved her mistress of Robinson Brown's attendance by kicking the Birdcatcher horse above the hock, they approached the osier-bed. It was bounded by the river on one side, the upper part of it being dry lying, of blackthorn, at the end of which was a strong, almost impracticable, fence, into a small meadow. At this end of the cover it was desirable that the crowd should assemble, and the hounds were brought round and thrown in there, as the best chance of affording a run. Charlie had taken his place at a corner of the cover indicated. He had scarcely forgotten Edith for a moment until now, when eyes and ears were straining for the hoped-for "gone away." The young lady, with more modesty than that exhibited by modern Amazons, had turned her horse back, and, walking along the hedgerow, had ridden through a gate into the meadow itself, partly to quiet her horse and partly to be out of the way. For a few minutes it had the desired effect, but almost immediately the hounds found;

a crash of melody ensued; the rate of the whips, the cheer of the huntsman, or the sudden rush of horsemen to some favoured spot, again upset the mare. At this moment, standing in his stirrups, and straining his eyes to catch sight of fox, or hounds, or anything but Edith Dacre, she recurred to his mind. He had seen her go back, and now, looking towards the meadow, through the fence, what was his distress to see the mare rearing and plunging wildly, as at every fresh bound she neared the river, swollen by autumnal rains. Edith kept her seat and her presence of mind, but she was deadly pale, and evidently her strength was going. A fresh blast of the horn and a " tally-ho back " brought more horses up at a hand gallop; the mare seized the bit in her teeth, and plunged madly towards the river's brink. And now everybody saw the danger and the impracticable nature of the fence, and galloped, Robinson Brown leading, towards the gate, some two hundred yards up the hedgerow. Almost as they started a terrible shriek broke on the ear; the mare reared bolt upright; the poor girl caught tight hold of the curb-rein, and in an instant more they both fell with a crash into the river. The mare extricated herself immediately; but there, on the waters, floated rapidly down stream the dark habit and brown tresses of that beautiful girl.

Charlie had quite forgotten the fox as soon as he perceived her situation on the bank; he hesitated only to calculate the possibility of clearing the fence, or of getting to the gate most quickly. The last scream and violent plunge of the mare decided the matter. His horse was raw, but fresh and resolute; the rails were strong, the fence pretty thick, but it allowed the pleasing vision of a broad, black ditch, and a second flight of timber on the other side. Catching hold of the reins in a grasp of iron, and sending both spurs into his horse's flanks, he rushed him at it. The result might be guessed: as Edith Dacre and the mare rolled off the bank into the water, Charlie Thornhill and his horse landed with a loud crash into the second flight of rails, which proved just strong enough to let them through, but with a heavy fall on the other side.

CHAPTER VII.

THE BEGINNING OF THE END.

"Strong reasons make strong actions."—*King John.*

CHARLIE, amongst other accomplishments, had learned to fall well. He was seldom seen running after his horse, over a ploughed field, with tearful entreaties to his friends to "tie him up at the next gate." He never let go the reins, as long as they remained unbroken, or was caught ignominiously endeavouring to soothe the cunning steed, who stands mildly grazing after having given his rider a fall that shakes every bone in his body, and leaves him with scattered limbs and senses to deplore his too-confiding reliance on a brute. The consequence was, that almost before he was down, he was up again; and with one short but heartfelt thanksgiving that *he* was not at this moment disabled, he dropped the reins which by instinct he held, and giving himself one shake, and one moment for

reflection, he ran towards the river to a point
somewhat below that at which Edith Dacre had
just risen to the surface. He saw she was free
from her horse, and that it was only a question
of how long it would take to saturate her heavy
riding - habit. As to assistance from the rest,
they were at this moment unhasping the gate
which had closed again, and were some three
hundred yards from the spot. Scarcely thirty
yards separated him from the object he loved
best on earth, or in the water, and in a second or
two he was at the river's brink. In two or three
vigorous strokes he was alongside of Edith, and
bearing her rapidly towards the angle formed
by the fence and the osier-bed, where landing
seemed easier than elsewhere. By the time he
reached the spot, Robinson Brown, Sir Thomas
Fallowtop, Mr. Dacre, pale as ashes, but covering
his emotion with an assumed calmness, two
young farmers, who had been waiting, out of the
crowd, with young horses, and about half a
dozen labouring men and boys, were ready to
give a hand or advice, as the case might be.
Charlie accepted the former, and disdained the
latter. Edith had already recovered in some

sort her consciousness, and was pouring out thanks, with eyes that told too truly how glad she was to be indebted to her deliverer. She clung to him, as he held her for one moment to his heart, and the next was in the arms of her father. He uttered not one word, but he looked conscious of the narrowness of her escape, and gave one short but sincere pressure of the hand to Charlie, which assured him that his share in the transaction was not forgotten. It is but justice to the field to say, that they were now about a mile from the cover in an opposite direction, the fox having broken at the very moment that Charlie charged the fence. According to received opinion, great men are in the habit of fixing their minds upon the business they are engaged in; and there is no doubt that a whole family might be drowned without exciting much surprise, or turning some men from the object they have in view. It is not therefore wonderful that Charlie should have been permitted the achievement of the present adventure without any interruption from the crowd, or any participator in his pleasure.

I have no doubt that, should the critics do me

the honour of noticing me some day or other, that they will not fail to point out the fortunate escape from drowning which has hitherto attended the Dacre family. What they may be inclined to predict of Mr. Edward Dacre's end, I can hardly say, beyond that he was not born to be drowned: a lady, I presume, will escape comment of that kind; but that an author should venture upon making his hero neither more nor less than a sort of rational Newfoundland, who lays claim to his mistress's gratitude, as much as her love, by his physical capability and his knowledge of swimming, shows a dearth of invention or imagination which ought to have restricted his pen to the narration of facts. But why should not two persons in one family have the misfortune to be nearly drowned? If such a thing were impossible, or even very uncommon, what a charming immunity for the young ladies would it be, that their brother should be the scapegoat; and that the girls should be born to a sort of immortality, because the boys of a family had broken every bone in each individual body. I might have written something infinitely more improbable. I might have followed this author

into the most mysterious depths of electro-
biology, or that into the superstitions of another
world, with the most perfect safety. But that
two members of the same family should have
escaped drowning by the same instrument or
agent, will appear incredible; and be branded,
I fear, by the critics, as an absurdity beneath
contempt.

But while I have been wandering, Edith
Dacre has been left dripping in her wet clothes
and wringing locks, now in the arms of her
father, and anon recomposing an extemporaneous
toilette, which had been deranged by the recent
immersion in the Floss. Ridicule is the
greatest enemy to love. Nothing is so trying
as an absurd position; but Charlie could see
nothing to laugh at in so providential an escape,
notwithstanding that a water nymph in a riding-
habit, and neat little Wellington boots, is pro-
vocative of some mirth. At another time, and
under other circumstances, he might have found
amusement in a contretemps which had deprived
a young woman of her hat, and brought down
all her back hair, dripping with water. At present, his object was shelter and warmth for the

poor girl, who had nearly fallen a victim to no unfeminine hardihood of her own, but to the unintentional thoughtlessness of her brother. I have seen ladies floating about in the water, self-immolated at the shrine of St. Hubert, but who were desirous of being considered upon all occasions pre-eminently capable of taking care of themselves.

Edith continued to shiver and shake, as well she might; and it became a question of how to get her home. At this juncture up came a groom of Mr. Dacre's, who had been left behind, at the house, in consequence of the increased number of guests, but who ought to have reached the cover earlier. It was suggested that he should ride Miss Dacre's mare, and that she should ride his horse; an arrangement easily made and equally agreeable to all parties, in the absence of a carriage, or any road to drive one. The saddles were changed, and more dead than alive she was lifted on to the groom's horse, fortunately a very quiet one. Charlie, as soon as the lady was in her saddle, declaring her capability to proceed, and the utter absence of any ill but that of fright and wet, made an inconvenient discovery for himself. His horse was lame: he had struck himself violently on the fetlock in his fall, and the standing still had given the joint time to become very stiff and painful. The next thing, therefore, was to displace the groom, which was done accordingly; and in spite of Edith's appeals, not to get on the mare, which were not the less tender for their sincerity, Charlie mounted the offender. He had but two regrets, that he had lost the run, and that Robinson Brown was escorting them home. It was a mixed feeling, but the last was by far the stronger of the two.

Gilsland was about two miles from the osier-bed; and as Edith had begun to shake off her faintness, after the sherry which had been forced upon her by the appeals of her father, and by the fortunate provision of Charlie's flask, it was proposed to jog on, as a means of keeping both Edith and Charlie from the effects of their ducking. In this manner they arrived at the Hall, and at once relieved Mrs. Dacre and Alice from any fears which an unprejudiced imagination is apt to attribute to a too early return from hunting, especially when accompanied by

such a development of back hair. The young
lady was dismissed to her room, where her
mother, sister, and two maids insisted upon
administering to her comforts, when she would
fain—oh! how fain!—have been alone, with
herself and her thoughts. For she had thanks
due to One whom neither her father nor Charlie
had quite forgotten at the moment, and in her
gratitude to the instrument, she could not help
reverting to the cause.

Mrs. Dacre's first idea was the true one, that
Charlie and Edith had been in the water
together ; and she knew that was often a prelude
to other misfortunes. She was very fond of
Charlie, but she did not like the idea of him
for a husband for one of her children. They
might look higher. Then she detected herself
making a compromise, and permitting herself
and her family the friendship of a detrimental.
There was a plausible excuse for that to the
world ; and Mrs. Dacre's world wanted an
apology for an imprudent marriage more than
that world where there will be none at all.
She found herself thinking more about Charlie's
uncle, his fortune, its extent, and his life. These

are what she called his prospects: the fact is
they were her own. Robinson Brown she could
not endure; but she rather thought that it would
be her duty to put up with a young man of such
immense expectations, and who had certainly
attracted the attention of several judicious ladies
of even higher ton than herself. Alice had long
suspected the state of Charlie's heart; she liked
him, for himself, and the debt of gratitude she
owed him for a brother and a sister, in all
probability would not remain the strongest link
that tied them together for any very long time.
She was sincerely glad of this, for she foresaw
the solution of the Gordian knot of *convenance*
cut by the preference he might claim for such
unequalled services. Mr. Dacre was an easy
person, not given to emotion, excepting in very
unexpected circumstances, such as we have detailed. He wrung Charlie's hand, as we have
seen; wished he could provide for him (abroad
perhaps!), and determined upon lending him
the mare, or one of his own horses, until his
own should be sound enough for him to ride.
He need not want a general invitation to Gilsland: *cela va sans dire.*

During the day the village Esculapius, Dr. Torrens, called. Nothing could be better than the young lady: "quiet; something light for dinner; a little soda-water, no wine, and the doctor would call again to-morrow." Doctor! thought Charlie, what in the name of fortune does the doctor want here? surely there's nothing the matter. Then came the curate: he returned to his duties without being introduced. Charlie hoped he was not coming on the morrow too. And then a message from the farm, to hope the young lady was not hurt. The answer was satisfactory enough. At that moment Mr. Robinson Brown, who had also been disappointed of his day's hunting, without, however, the satisfaction which accompanied Charlie's disappointment, lounged into the room. Robinson Brown dabbled in polite literature, as he imagined, so he picked up a magazine, whilst Charlie looked out of the window, struggling to get the better of a rather bad fit of the spleen. Alice was with her sister; and she was his only sedative in the house. The fact is that love, of which he had taken a strong dose, did not agree with Charlie's temper.

" Why, Thornhill, I thought you were gone to Van Diemen's Land, or Heligoland, or some land or other in Africa. I was quite agreeably surprised to see you yesterday at dinner," said Mr. Brown, with a comfortable kind of patronage in his tone.

"No, not yet. When do you go ? " rejoined the other, rather tartly.

" Gwacious ! what a fellow you are ! Why should *I* go to those outlandish places ? I don't want to be eaten alive, my dear fellow," said the cornet.

" Oh ! nobody 'll eat you alive."

" I don't know: 'pon my soul I don't know about that. I'm not so tough as you think for, Thornhill." He was soft enough, to do him justice.

" No ; but a man may be very soft, and yet disagree with a fellow," rejoined Charlie; and, having delivered himself of this sentiment, he turned again to the window. He was not fated to enjoy his repose long, for he was once more interrupted by the Plunger.

" You're weeding, eh, Thornhill ? weeding, I understand; and that sort of thing ? "

" What? a garden or a stud? I've weeded the latter pretty closely."

" No, no; not weeding, but weeding," said dear Jane : " weeding with a coach, you know." He made rather a violent struggle to make himself comprehensible.

" Yes; I am reading for a commission," replied Charlie, turning once more to the contemplation of the black clouds, which portended a wet ride home for the sportsmen.

" Aw—aw—yes—great baw weeding, to some fellaws. Now we never had any examination, or that sort of thing, when I went into the service; nothing of the kind," persevered Robinson Brown.

" So I should think," said Charlie, who saw it would be polite to say something.

" Our fellows are aw—aw—so ignowant : not bad fellows, you know, but so infernally ignowant."

" So I should have imagined," replied Charlie once more, who was watching a figure intently which appeared at the further end of the shrubbery, and which exhibited every appearance of one of the ladies of the house walking briskly to and fro. "So I should have imagined."

"Oh! you know our fellows, then. Do you ever dine at the mess? Bad cook; and altogether—aw—aw—that sort of thing. Do you know Carnaby?"

"No; I only know you." And just as Robinson Brown was recommencing on some other subject, Charlie, feigning an unexpected reminiscence, rushed out of the room in search of the shawl, which had once more disappeared round the shrubbery. It was Alice Dacre.

Charlie was not a bold man; and there was no one in the house at that time, excepting, perhaps, Lady Elizabeth, to avoid whom he would not have gone a mile round. But as soon as he saw that it was Alice Dacre he testified an invincible desire for news of Edith. What more natural? says the reader. What more proper? say I. And yet, from the moment it occurred to him, it seemed to possess insuperable objections. It took a long time to come to the point; and then it is doubtful whether the attractions of Alice would have sufficed to draw him out, but for the repulsion of Mr. Robinson Brown.

"What a morning it has been for us, Mr. Thornhill," began Alice, who exhibited very recent traces of tears, which did not escape the discriminating eyes of Charlie. "Poor Edith! it has been too much for her: and, now that the excitement is over, the reaction is very painful. And what do we not owe you?"

"Don't let that burden you, Miss Dacre."

"It does not burden us; but——" And here poor Alice blushed, for she knew one whom it did burden painfully, and another she guessed at, who hugged her burden closer than was good for her. Alice Dacre was very thoughtful for others. "Oh! Mr. Thornhill, I could say so much. If you knew how we have lived together, and what a blessing you have restored to us all by your courage;" and here a good large pearl did run over. But she soon brightened again, for she saw that the conversation was painful to Charlie, who was not inclined to magnify his own exploit, though he was not blind to the danger of the girl.

Alice felt a strong inclination to ask after his brother; but as the words rose they stuck; and she only asked him where he was going to spend his winter.

"I scarcely know; I presume at Thornhills. But, you know, I am reading, and must work hard at Scampersdale; for I hope to have a commission before long." Charlie wondered where he was likely to be quartered.

"Yes, we heard of that; but you did talk of going to Melton."

"I did; but I have not time. What hunting I do I must do in this neighbourhood. However, I must be a prisoner for a fortnight or more. I lamed my horse."

"And papa proposes to send over one of his, or the mare Edith rode to-day, if you think her worth riding."

"I hope we shall see Edith at dinner," said Charlie.

"No, not at dinner to-day. To-morrow Dr. Torrens proposes calling early; and I hope she will be much better. But, tell me, when does the steeple-chase between your brother's horse and Mr. Robinson Brown's Reluctance come off? Edith will want all the news."

"Not immediately; it's postponed. And as I am to ride, I should like to have got through my literary difficulties before I risk your sister's gloves; for I know she has backed the horse. But," added he, encouragingly, " I think we can manage to win."

" I hope so; òr poor Edith will be ruined in gloves. I heard her backing you to her last penny; so I beg you win."

" Shall we see her at dinner to-day? You fear not. But is anything the matter? Tell me, tell me, Miss Dacre." And here, seeing how far his feelings had carried him away, he became suddenly cold, and hoped it was nothing but fatigue. " Had they much opinion of their doctor?"

" Oh! yes; certainly. He was to see Edith to-morrow; and if she had a good night she would be better, no doubt." And with this Charlie was obliged to be satisfied.

But the next morning Edith was much the same. She was to lie in bed and to keep her room throughout the day. The excitement had been too much for her.

Sickness in a house full of guests is always very depressing. Nobody seems to know what to do. There is a vague listlessness about the visitors, and the most nearly interested have time for nothing. There is a constant energy pervades them all. Breakfast is a scurry; luncheon is not cheerful, and wants the plans and the proposals of a healthy time; as to dinner, you have to sit down with a vacant chair or two. Then one drops in, then another; every one has come from the sick-chamber. You feel your insignificance and uselessness. You can do nothing, and are plainly *de trop*. Under these circumstances was the party at Gilsland. So on the Monday morning Charlie returned to work; but he had the happiness of seeing Mr. Robinson Brown depart before him, a woe-begone object of simulated tenderness. He assumed that hangdog style as a privilege; and Charlie did not know well what to do with himself where, in proportion to the tenderness of his feelings, he was compelled to appear the least interested of any. Robinson Brown, however, once gone, he started for Captain Armstrong's with allayed temper and relieved mind.

CHAPTER VIII.

LIFE IN THE SHIRES.

" Things sweet to taste prove in digestion sour."—*Richard II.*

CHARLIE found himself at Captain Armstrong's, once more involved in the intricacies of English spelling, French dictation, the square root, and simple equations; and why called simple he had some difficulty in understanding. He had received a note from Alice Dacre three days later, which gave but a very poor account of Edith's recovery; and when he rode over on Saturday morning to inquire after her, ostensibly to see his young horse, it was impossible to conceal the fact of very severe illness. In truth, she was attacked by low fever, the result of cold and excitement combined; and a summons for a more reliable opinion than that of Dr. Torrens confirmed Charlie's fears of considerable danger. During three weeks of much suffering, alternating between life and death, he was as little

able to pursue any efficient study almost as she
would have been; and it was not till the fourth
week that his mind was made easy by an
assurance, on a repeated visit, that all danger
was completely over, and that beef-tea and champagne were doing the work of the doctor in
curing, not in killing, as might be supposed.

Leaving Edith to get well, and Charlie to
recover his lost ground, I take this opportunity
for a reflection or two, which the reader can
miss, if he likes, but which is as much the
necessary ingredient of a novel as pepper of a
rabbit-pie. Indeed, a novel which deals in
characters, facts, or fictions, as the case may
be, and nothing else, is not unlike one of those
excellent Strasbourg patés from which nothing
has been omitted but the truffles and the
seasoning. And though I have no doubt it
would be swallowed, if fashion gave the word, as
many a novel is read, without a syllable to give
it flavour beyond its details, I cannot imagine
that persons of real taste would approve it.

It will have been observed that Edith Dacre
was a lively, cheerful, high-spirited girl, with
some little vanity and love of display, but many

lovable qualities. Her anxiety to ride an
unruly mare arose partly from this circumstance
and partly from sheer animal spirits. A good
ducking would have been sufficient punishment,
if any were thought necessary; but a fever, which
reduced her to a skeleton, frightened her family,
nearly killed her lover with anxiety, and deprived
her for a time of a valuable head of hair, seems
to have been more than adequate. What shall
we say of the young ladies of the present day,
who are not satisfied with a modest exhibition of
themselves at the cover side, but who are either
so desirous of display, or so wedded to the
charms of manly exercise, as to pride themselves
upon the successful negotiation of stiff timber or
fourteen feet of water? whose conversation has
become a mixture of the stable and the school-
room, and whose fantastic dress ranges between
the collars and pea-jacket of a Whitechapel gent
and the picturesque conventionalities of a rope-
dancer? What is the reason of all this? Who
or what are the ladies who have introduced this
furore cavalleresco amongst the most lovely, the
most delicate, the most womanlike of the women
of this world? Alas! "how are the mighty

fallen," and the insignificant exalted! Who ever
heard of them thirty years ago, save at some
unholy Bacchanalian festival? Were their names,
or abodes, or calling the subject of conversation
to our mothers? Who were the men who within
the last thirty years kissed the tips of their
fingers to mysterious broughams in the presence
of mothers, sisters, or the women destined to be
their wives? Who are to regenerate the men of
this wicked world but the women? And are
they to do it by winking at their follies and
applauding in public their unrefined inclina-
tions? Is it to be done by jokes, innuendos, and
doubles entendres, and a levity which takes for its
subject the most sacred relation between man
and woman, to hold it up to derision, or to deny
its sanctity? " Pretty horsebreakers," forsooth !
Pretty hearth and hope breakers ! If men and
women agreed to call things by their right
names, we *could* hear but little of them from
woman's lips. For "quod fædum est factu,
idem est turpe dictu." In the general silence
proclamatory of their condemnation they would
lose their effrontery; and what asks for toleration
secretly would cease to be talked about openly.

Now they have excited a curiosity which is neither seemly nor useful: public print-shops are decorated with their portraits; photography hands down their turpitude to a still more vicious generation; their carriages are known, their horses are coveted, their opera-boxes are the objects of *lorgnettes* from every side, and impunity and observation stamp their effrontery with the seal of fashion. That society, which, in the vindication of its rights and virtue, refuses its hand to one who has erred, but who has retrieved her position, as far as may be, by marriage and a life of modest utility, sanctions luxurious youth in the prosecution of vice, and gives to the most immodest declaration of unchastity a charm which is denied to suffering virtue or newly adopted respectability. Yes! reader, you who hate sentimentality may not be averse to decency and truth. Miss it, if you will, and go on with the story: but if you care about the honour and spotless purity of your own women, the women of your own hearth and country, read it, and lay it to your heart.

And what of Tom Thornhill all this time? He was at it, body and soul. A dozen horses at

Melton; a house that befitted his ample means;
and companions that drank deep of the cup in
which he pledged them.   There was nothing but
pleasure before him, and he revelled in the
prospect. . And in that prospect was one form
which enhanced the beauty of the picture, and
stood out part and parcel of a grand and striking
foreground.   Alice Dacre, with her glossy hair,
and soft black eyes, and truthful serenity—not
severity.   Of that there was none.   There was
force and character, but without one drawback.
Yes, one.   Alice was too confident of her own
discernment; and when men did not turn out
what she, in her own mind, had made them, she
was disappointed, and failed to see the good in
them which her unprejudiced opinion might
have done.   But there she stood in Tom Thornhill's picture of future happiness, bright and
glorious, for whom he would have sacrificed
himself, but not all; not his passion, his
devourer, his god.   He could—strange infatua-
tion!—have thrown his thousands into the sea
for her sake, and turned on his heel a beggar
with Alice by his side; but he could not
relinquish the thousands of other people, to

bask for ever in the sunshine of her love. Did
he 'know this ? did he ask his conscience if it
were so ? And what answer would it have
returned ?

The fact is, Tom Thornhill had too much to
do to ask his conscience anything; and his
conscience was becoming of that hard cut-and-
dried character, as to be almost shy of answering
anything in its former straightforward manner.
It had got a fine polish on it; and, instead of the
roughness of inherent truth, it gave nothing
more than the reflection of him who looked into
it. It was very like a looking-glass, and would
have answered flatteringly enough. What a
comfortable life it was to be sure, and how it
tended to give elasticity to the morals, and
compression to philanthropy ? Breakfast at
——; bless me, where are the hounds to-
morrow ? Grilled bones, devilled kidneys, a
boar's head, and a very well prepared réchauffé
of fish ! A gallop or phaeton to Ranksborough,
Kirby Gate, Six Hills, or Great Glen ! The
cheerful greetings on the road, or at the cover
side; and the cigar, so pleasant in the still
sullen air of a November morning. And then

the day's work: the rattling burst of twenty
minutes; the cooler hunting over a cold plough,
where every hound has to hold his own, and
where the quickly-breathing horses that have
gone the run may catch their wind, or be handed
over to the second horseman, who has waited for
the nick. The afternoon fox, so often proving
a straight one; when the eagerness of the too
impetuous sportsman has had time to cool; when
hounds are not pressed by a too willing field;
and when the true workman finds the value of
his morning's self-denial. All these things Tom
was enjoying in their veriest perfection. Who
had better horses than Thornhill? Nobody.
Who rode them straighter? Nobody. Who
had a better cook, a better cellar, a better
digestion? Who was a luckier fellow than he?
Halte-là! Had he satisfied himself with this,
who should have said me "nay"? But there
were other pleasures not so cheerful, not so
innocent, not so happy in their termination.

A good table is one of the essentials of a
gentleman. I do not know that a gentleman
enjoys a good dinner more than other people;
frequently his own tastes are simple in the

extreme. Soup, fish, grouse, and a cabinet
pudding, a glass or two of Burgundy, and a
bottle of claret, is a dinner for a prince. Some
like a haunch of venison, others one slice from a
roast leg of mutton; but it does not behove a
man of fashion to forget that his friends may
have a more discriminating taste than his own.
But a few thousands a year go a great way in the
pleasures of sense. There is but one thing that
no fortune can resist: the gaming-table. Tom
loved play, and he loved to play high. Hitherto
he had had but few opportunities of indulging
his passion to any great extent—in private. He
had backed horses, however, with a recklessness
that was the result of strong prejudice or
ignorance, and had already suffered. At this
game he stood no chance of winning, excepting
by accident. He was always playing a game
which they with whom he played knew better
than himself. He betted as honestly, and paid
as readily, and with the same good humour, as he
did everything. But he did not always get paid;
so that, like the zero, *cæteris paribus*, there was
an eternal pull against him. He had already
been raising money; and it was clear that in a

few years he must be in the hands of the Jews.
That scattered but worm-gathering people had
their eyes upon him, as one of their daintiest
morsels. They had tried Lord Carlingford, and
found him unripe for their gathering; the Punter
was not worth the trouble. Cressingham paid
too regularly; when he wanted money, there were
no renewals, no bonds; they saw no fish so ready
to take the bait as Tom Thornhill. Already
they counted their 60 per cent., and something
tangible—Thornhills—to fall back upon.

The antecedents of Wilson Graves were not
good. We know that in the tragedy of Fred
Ludlow he played an ugly part: but he was
always well received in society, and the stain
rested only on his name, not on his company.
Besides, had he not a good prospective property
from his uncle, Lord Slangsbury? And what will
not that cover? A multitude of his own sins, if
none of anybody else's. About this time he
arrived in the Quorn country, with a stud of
weight-carrying horses which would have entitled
him to some respect, if nothing else would do so.
He had never been intimate with the Thornhills.
He was not exactly in the same set; but he was

not easily passed over in the company of hard-riding and hard-drinking men who came toge-ther, after a good day's sport, round Thornhill's table.

"Who was that we left swimming about in the Whissendine to-day with our second fox?" asked Captain Charteris of Lord Carlingford, as they sat in Thornhill's drawing-room in their hunting things before a roasting fire, with no other light but its ruddy and cheerful blaze. "He looked to me as if he stood a good chance of being drowned."

"Only Wilson Graves," said his lordship; "he went very well up to that. But I could see his horse didn't mean to have the water; he became exceedingly shifty as soon as he caught sight of it, and I heard him go in just as I landed with a desperate scramble; and when I looked round, I saw nothing but a hat and one top-boot above the water; I presume they belonged to him. I suppose he got out?"

"Yes," said Charteris; "I pulled up a moment, and he scrambled to the bank. The water was not above four feet and a half deep there, so he was perfectly safe. Is he the man that broke the bank at Homburg the year before last, and got out of window with twenty thousand dollars from a Broadway billiard-room, whilst the indignant Yankee was sharpening his bowie-knife at the bottom of the stairs?"

"So they say," rejoined Lord Carlingford; "he gave Langton five-and-twenty pounds to toss him up for five hundred, one night, at the door of his own house—by the hall-lamp—and won. Langton did not want to toss; but he thought the odds justified him in accepting the challenge; and when he turned round, there was nobody there to hedge."

"Perhaps he'll make you the same offer to-night," said Tom Thornhill, who had just come in from the stable; "he's coming to dinner to-day. I've given him a bed, as he hunts on this side to-morrow; and it saves him a ride back to Leicester. Not a bad thing to-day; and that new horse of Joe Anderson's carried me very well."

"He's a thoroughbred one, is he not?"

"Yes, quite; and that's what makes him so good through dirt; if they have but limbs there's nothing like them in difficulties."

"By-the-bye, Thornhill, has anything more been done about the match between your brown

horse and Robinson Brown's mare ? It ought to
be coming off soon."

"It's postponed by agreement for another
month. Charlie thinks he shall ride so much
lighter when his examination is over, and
Robinson Brown's mare wasn't fit, I believe. So
he wanted to have it later in the season."

"I think 12 st. is always 12 st., examination
or not ; and I shouldn't have postponed it. I
suppose your horse is fit." Thus spake Captain
Charteris, who no doubt was quite right, and
whose sagacity will be applauded by the racing
men and betting fraternity in general. In fact,
as Wilson Graves that day explained at table, it
was very doubtful whether Thornhill had any
right to postpone the match, as the brown horse
had become the favourite, and might now be
considered the property of the British public.

"I haven't seen him, but my trainer writes me
word that he never looked better in his life. I
believe they will lay 3 to 1 on him before the day
of the race. But I didn't want to rob the poor
devil, if his mare wasn't fit to go." Thus spake
Tom Thornhill, with the spirit of a gentleman
and a sportsman, but with more of the innocence

of the dove than the wiliness of the serpent. It was not long before he got the better of these weaknesses, to a certain extent, though they would cling to him more or less to the end of his life.

"If you fellows are going to dine here to-day, I should advise you to go and dress." And with that he walked out of the room.

Perhaps the really pleasantest time after hunting is that shadowy, idle, dreaming hour or two in front of the fire, which may be passed before dressing, either, as I have endeavoured to describe it, in uninteresting chat, in a happy state of semi-somnolence, or in the pages of the most stirring and eventful novel to be met with. The first two states are preferable, as demanding no attention, levying no tax on the intelligence whatever; whilst the last, too frequently calling for a great stretch of the imagination, or a wonderful amount of credulity, is the most appetising. I know nothing so comfortable as the nap, for my part; and it has the double advantage of present repose and additional vigour for the evening's campaign.

"Pass the claret-jug here, Graves, if you please:

we'll have some more when that's gone. It's not true that old Lexington has bolted with Lady Mary Teasdale, is it? for I heard so to-day."

"Not a word of truth in it. He's in bed with the gout, and very hard up, so he ordered himself to be denied to everybody. As he was not seen, and she disappeared about the same time, naturally they were supposed to have disappeared together. You know his horses are for sale next Monday fortnight?"

"What! from his attack: is it so severe as that?" said Lord Carlingford, who was a connection of the gouty peer, and had some expectations.

"No, certainly not, Lord Carlingford," said Wilson Graves; "his attack is on the chest: they say he had lost forty thousand at the end of last season, and that he dropped fifteen more to a Russian countess at Spa just before the beginning of the winter. Lord Lexington and the count were the best of friends, and everything seemed to be arranged upon the most amicable footing."

"There was a story current that an Englishman shared in the plunder," said Charteris, somewhat abruptly.

"Do you believe it?" asked Wilson Graves as abruptly, at the same time with colour heightened by claret or temper.

"That would depend entirely upon who should deny it." The conversation was taking an unpleasant turn, which it would have required a little tact to stop, when the dining-room door was thrown open, and Mr. Robinson Brown, junior, was announced.

Now be it known to the reader that Robinson Brown was not a favourite with Tom Thornhill, nor, indeed, with any of the men who were present. But Tom was hospitality itself, and could no more do an unkind action, or allow any one to think himself aggrieved in his house, than he could fly. So down sat "Dear Jane" with as hearty a welcome as if it had been Charlie himself.

"Where are you from?" "What horses have you with you?" "Where are you staying?" "Seen any sport?" were questions poured in upon him as fast as the claret was poured out for him.

"I'm just come from the Dacres," said he, with considerable pride at the announcement of a name which gave him a favourable status in the present company.

"The Dacres? by Jove!" said Tom. "Any news? Old Dacre pretty well? Capital fellow! 'pon my soul. And the girls?" added he, after a pause, not liking to appear over anxious. "Who had you, there?"

"Oh! yes, all very well, excepting Miss Dacre: she's ill of a howwid fever." He had no time to finish the sentence, for Tom was on his feet in a moment; and, fortunately for him, down went the claret-jug, which attracted immediate attention, whilst he had time to collect himself. But the effort was a strong one, and left Tom burning hot, with a very uncomfortable degree of fever himself, whilst his informant added, "Yaas, the younger one, Edith. Charles Thornhill fished her out of the water—fell in near Dacre's osier-bed the end of last week; your bwother lamed his horse. "Vewy unfortunate altogether, wasn't it?" And he really felt as much as he was capable of feeling: for he had managed to get up what he called a good wholesome passion for the little Dacre. Tom's colour had subsided, and by the time the butler had brought another bottle of claret the excitement was over, though Tom continued to repeat, " Poor girl! 'Pon my soul, sorry to hear that : very. And how's Charlie ? "

"Your bwother? Oh! he's vewy well. Wather sweet in that quarter, I should say." And here Mr. Robinson Brown lapsed into unusual insipidity. It was getting late, and, as no one took any more claret, they adjourned to the drawing-room.

Here Carlingford yawned ; Robinson Brown stretched himself on a sofa ; Cressingham hummed an air out of a new opera of the last season ; Charteris picked up the " Racing Calendar ; " Wilson Graves feigned sleep in an arm-chair ; and Thornhill himself walked straight to the card-tables. " Anybody for a rubber ? " Nobody answered. " Graves, have a rubber ? " And a game was made, at which Tom Thornhill won. So far, so good. Then they tried hazard. This was not so good for Tom, who began to lose, and, like a true gambler, backed his bad luck. Brown took his leave after having suc-

ceeded in backing his mare for the match. The
day was then fixed for it to come off, and the
riders were declared. Mr. Robinson Brown
would steer his own mare, and Mr. Charles
Thornhill would ride for his brother. Men
naturally asked, Why should Mr. Thornhill not
ride himself? Because he had a handsome
rent-roll, and his brother had none. And so
the night wore on. By degrees the men moved
off, Carlingford to his rooms, Cressingham to
his, and all to give orders about the morrow.
And then, instead of going to bed, Tom Thornhill would play. His iron constitution seemed
to know no fatigue : his indomitable passion was
only roused by losses. Nor was Wilson Graves
the man to thwart his purpose. One word
might then have checked him : but there was
no one to say, " No, hang it, Thornhill, we've
had enough for to-night; let's go to bed." The
devil had taken possession of the room, in the
shape of a dice-box, and his prime minister was
Wilson Graves. So they went to it again, the
one with well-dissembled satisfaction, the other
with unfeigned enjoyment—an enjoyment which
never appeared to diminish with the loss of hun-

dreds. But at last the game did flag, from a sort of inherent deference to received opinion, that men ought to go to bed before three who have to start for the cover-side again at half-past nine ; so they took up their flat candlesticks, and prepared to go, leaving behind them a curious testimony to the housemaid of their evening's occupation : empty soda-water bottles, the ends of cigars, three or four packs of cards, a backgammon board, and a dice-box.

"What do you think about the match now, Thornhill ? That ass Mr. Brown seems to have a tolerable opinion of his chance ; he laid out another two hundred at evens, when he went away, with your friend Captain Charteris."

"I can lay four to three on myself," said Thornhill, running his eye down a betting-book which he took from his coat-tail pocket. "I can lay 800*l.* to 600*l.*, if that will suit you."

"Make it 800*l.* to 500*l.*," said Wilson Graves : "it's more than I like, but I can get rid of half upon those terms. You know nothing but a 'dead 'un' can rob you of it."

"Give me 50*l.*, and I'll do it," said Tom, booking the bet, and walking straight up-stairs some five hundred pounds lighter than when he came down them at seven o'clock.

And so life wagged in Melton under the reign of King Tom.

"That will do, Johnson. Leave that coat and waistcoat out; the morning looks stormy," said Mr. Wilson Graves, some days after the above occurrence, to his valet; "I shall not want you any more. Send up George." And the gentleman proceeded to put a finishing touch to his toilet.

"Come in," said he, a few minutes later, in answer to a knock at the door; "come in:" and enter George, the most perfect specimen of a confidential groom. He was ready for starting, and clearly imagined that his summons had something to do with preparation, for he held in one hand a neat but useful hunting-whip, in the other a hat brushed to within an inch of its very existence: not a hair was out of place either on it or on the head to which it belonged. His features were regular, straight, and hard. His eye was expressive of nothing whatever, and his mouth of nothing but discretion. He kept it shut most resolutely. He had a furtive

glance which betokened at all times a suspicion
that the door ought to be locked, and, though
looking straight before him, it was clear he
could see the handle. His ears always appeared
to be at cross purposes, one laid back, and the
other straight in front *in utrumque paratus*,
ready for either side. He was a first-rate groom,
and an admirable second horseman.

"Who goes on this morning with The
Miller?" demanded the master.

"Job Shuffles, sir," replied the man.

"And who rides The Mannikin?"

"I do, sir." Here he changed legs, and,
seeing one hair out of place on his hat, gave it
an elaborate polish with his right arm.

"Do you know that brown horse of Mr. Thornhill's, that he has matched against Reluctance,
Mr. Robinson Brown's mare?" again said the
master, finishing off a neat and successful tie,
and looking his man very straight in the face.

"The big brown os, as Mr. Thornhill rode
last year, and hung up the field at Gopsall Park
paling? Oh! yes, sir, I know the os well
enough. He's down at Sam Downy's, in training
for this match : leastways, I hear so."

"Very likely. Do you know Downy?" And
here Wilson Graves dropped his voice to little
above a whisper.

"His son and me was schoolfellows, and in
service together, when I lived first with Lord
Ambulance, sir; and I generally go down to
the old man's every year for a day or two,
just for a change of air, and a little quiet or so,
after the season here, see his osses out, and
help him a bit with the stud." Here George
pulled up his neckcloth, and seemed to imply
that he was rather a valuable coadjutor to old
Downy.

"Can you give him some advice about the
brown horse, then, George? I know you're a
clever fellow, and can do what you like. That
horse musn't win; in fact, he can't win: the
mare's the one to back." And here Mr. Wilson
Graves condescended to look again at his groom
in a very peculiar manner, which said, "You
know which horse the money is on now, so do
your possible to bring it off."

"They're uncommon sweet, sir; they love
the brown os like theirselves: and as to the
Squire, they love him amost as well as the os."

"And I tell you what they love better than the brown horse, or the Squire, and that's money." Graves judged the world by his own standard: he loved money's worth, and cared little how he got it.

"I don't know, sir; you know best: but it's a dangerous game among that lot." George looked preternaturally solemn, and as innocent as a dove.

"It's not the first time we've had to deal with danger. The boy's a certainty, if you bid high enough. Pull the string strong, and they'll all dance. It's time to be off; give me my coat, and send round the hack at half-past nine."

George gave what he intended to be a smile of intelligence, but which was not responded to by his master, and left the room.

CHAPTER IX.

AN OFFER.

"Marriage is honourable in all."

"Set a thief to catch a thief!" I think not. The two would be just as likely to combine to rob you, and you would meet with the amount of sympathy you deserve. I cannot understand the principle upon which the greatest poacher in the county makes the best gamekeeper. Surely there are plenty of honest men, with the same amount of knowledge in the destruction of vermin and the preservation of game; and, if so, no gentleman is justified in preferring successful roguery to honourable industry. I am not anxious to see our country police chosen from amongst our ticket-of-leave men, and should certainly mistrust the inspector from Portland Island or the *bagnes*. Not so Wilson Graves. His retainers were not selected for honourable antecedents; and, as their work was sometimes dirty, the instruments were to be not over-scrupulous. Men who live by their wits in a small way, work for themselves, and their operations are on a par with their expectations. Men who must have thousands out of nothing are the great villains of society; who keep in pay a host of artisans, agents of evil devices, the diggers and delvers after the philosopher's stone.

Graves cared very little whom his people robbed, as long as they let him go scot-free. To say truth, his own rascalities were so numerous, that he gave them very little time to idle. George Ritsom, his groom, was his prime minister; he selected him because he was clever, unscrupulous, and walked about with a rope round his neck, and his master knew it. He was therefore his very humble servant, and understood a hint as well as most men whose apprehensions are quickened by the fear of a halter. It was not quite so bad as that, however; still men have been hung for the same and for less. He had once poisoned a horse; and the proofs were in the hands of Wilson Graves. Good heavens! what a life to lead. I do not speak of either as an absolute pleasure, but better far would it be to be hanged at once, honestly and like a gentleman, than to go through the world the slave of such a man as he. However, there was nothing between servitude to the devil and utter ruin, so George set about his task with a will, and not without hopes, by corruption of an honest lad, of a successful termination. Both master and man acted upon a dictum of Sir Robert Walpole's, that " every man had his price ;" by which this world was reduced to the condition of a huge slave market, in which it was supposed that every man must be possessed of some demon, which rules him with a rod of iron under the semblance of a golden thread. I need hardly say, for the credit of human nature, that the dogma is as false as it is dangerous.

Whilst Tom Thornhill was enjoying himself, hunting, losing his money, making good resolutions, and breaking them, and Wilson Graves was profiting by his lengthened visit in Melton, Charlie had three things on his mind which caused him considerable anxiety. The first was his examination, which, as it approached, presented its difficulties in gigantic proportions; the second was Edith Dacre, about whom and whose

love he felt as most modest men in his position
would have felt; for, like many a brave, true-
hearted fellow, he had but small reliance upon his
own powers of pleasing. He knew what a prize
she was, and his love, as it magnified her value,
magnified the temptation it held out to other
men. He had difficulty in believing that she
could be seen without being admired, or that the
fruit could hang long enough on the tree to abide
his gathering. Charlie had a great deal of true
chivalry in his nature. He was rough, shy,
almost awkward in women's society, but with a
feeling for their weakness which is rare indeed
amongst your lady-killers. He was not blind to
the fact of his claims upon her gratitude; and
since her recovery, he had been made to understand, by constant kindness, how thoroughly her
family appreciated his services. But this was to
him an additional bar to his advancement; and
he was further than ever from making her
understand his feelings towards her, if such an
idea had ever entered his mind. Charlie was
one of those men who could no more have told a
woman he loved her, premeditatedly, than he
could have committed sacrilege with his eyes

open. In the present case he looked upon the
two things as very much alike. So he made
himself uncomfortable, to his full satisfaction;
which he need not have done had he known all I
knew. The third care was not a heavy one, for
his confidence here was as great as in the other
matters it was small. This was the steeple-chase
between the brown horse, which went commonly
by the name of Œdipus—from a certain fulness
about one of his fetlocks, but which was simply a
callous swelling from a blow when a yearling—
and the mare Reluctance, the property of his
mortal enemy, Robinson Brown. He was very
jealous of that young man—not without cause.
For when we take into consideration a fashionable
lisp, or whatever his peculiarity of pronunciation
might be called, a quantity of first-class jewellery,
the whitest of hands, and neatest of feet, a tall,
delicate figure, Mr. Poole's very best attentions,
and the enormous fortune to which he was heir,
what young woman could resist him? Yet Edith
Dacre managed to do so in a very decided
manner. And whilst Charlie was fretting, under
a whole suit of flannel and three top-coats every
morning, at the fancied success of that individual

in his pursuit, and which added immensely to the effect of the aforesaid flannels, in getting him down to the requisite 12 st. 4 lb. with the saddle and bridle, John Robinson Brown, the heir apparent, was smarting, not from rejected love, but injured vanity. Charlie Thornhill's slashing performance, and consequent rescue of Edith Dacre, with the very warm feeling which was exhibited towards him by every member of the Dacre family, had so roused the dormant energies of the Plunger, that he was determined upon closing the account at once. An opportunity soon presented itself.

No sooner was Miss Edith's health perfectly re-established, which it was in a few weeks, from the excellence of her constitution and the invincibility of her spirits, than she determined upon riding again. She began with the old pony, and prudently confined herself at first to the road. It was not long, however, before a lovely morning, such as we have only occasionally in the winter, tempted her to the cover-side. Her father and Mr. John Robinson Brown were her escort. The latter of the two rode one of his very best-looking horses, and was altogether such a pattern

of perfection as no one but the best of tailors
and the most skilful of valets ever sent out.
Edith's charms at the breakfast-table, her lovely
figure, the glow of renewed health, and the
simple beauty of her unaffected toilette, had
completely upset her lover. Mr. Dacre was
joined on his way to the meet, but a short
distance off, by one of his turnip-growing friends,
who had got him fast upon the subject of swedes
and parsneps making admirable soup, and the
relative proportions of saccharine matter in the
one or the other. The horses were at a foot's
pace, as the gentlemen rode their hunters, and
accommodated themselves to their fair companion's humour. She and the millionnaire were
about a hundred yards behind, and their conversation had taken a turn on general affairs, and
affairs of the heart in particular. Never was
such a chance, thought the knight; such a thing
never can be going to happen, the lady would
have thought, had she thought about it. She
was just then wondering who the friend was
whom he was describing as "weally vewy much
—aw—aw—positively quite unable—aw—aw, one
of the most wwetched, or the most fortunate—aw

—of beings, sufferwings, and that sort of thing quite widiculous, mawwiage, and so forth, difficult to expwess his feelings,"—when, leaning gently forward, he ventured to place his own ungloved hand on the lady's pommel of the sadde, occupied already by the tightly-gloved one of Edith Dacre. At that moment a cheerful little bird in the hedgerow (a "wobin in fact," as he afterwards described it), who had heard every word, and understood it—which is more than I or you could have done—flew out with a twitter right in front of Robinson Brown's horse. Captain Bobadil, who was fresher than usual (and he had an awkward way of putting up his back sometimes), gave one lurch to the off-side, as the gallant cornet was leaning down a little too tenderly, shot out his hind legs with a peculiar twist of the back, and sent his master right into the mud at the pony's feet. Having done this, he trotted on in magnificent form to join the turnip-crushers in front, who were thus made aware of the little accident behind. If Robinson Brown wanted an answer to his remarkable proposal, he found it in an uncontrollable fit of laughter, which the poor girl nearly strangled

herself in her endeavour to stifle. The only
result to him was the kind inquiries of his
friends at the cover-side, whether he had been
larking on the way to the meet; and some
sapient remarks, that when he was older he'd
know better. The robin evidently knew all
about it; for he saved Edith Dacre, what is
always a painful performance to a good-hearted
girl, the necessity of refusing a great ass, like a
lady. How she would have got through it she
has not the slightest idea to this day. He never
began again.

Of course the thing was not mentioned by
the two parties concerned. We can scarcely
conceive Mr. Robinson Brown publishing his
own defeat. I can answer for Edith Dacre's
silence. In the beginning of December, however, there was a four days' frost, and men came
up to town.

"By Jove, Lurcher, how d'ye do?" said our
old acquaintance, Tuftenham, of the Foreign
Office, walking into the Reform one morning,
and tapping his friend on the shoulder. "What
sport?"

"Fair; not very first-rate," replied the other,

"We've killed about twenty brace of foxes. Payne has had some capital sport in the Pytchley country. Any news in town?"

"Not much," said the Government clerk. "You know Robinson Brown, the man in the 103rd Dragoon Guards?"

"The woman, you mean," interposed Lurcher.

"He proposed to Edith Dacre, out riding. You know the Dacre, Teddy's sister? and she knocked him off his horse."

"I beg your pardon, Tuftenham," said young Balderdash of the Blues. "I had it from a man who saw it. They were going to cover when it happened; and Charlie Thornhill, who thought he had insulted her in some way, pulled him off his horse. The thing was hushed up, because of the girl. By-the-way," added he, lowering his tone confidentially, "don't mention it, for it was told me as a great secret, and it might create a row if it got wind—fellows are so deuced particular about that sort of thing."

"Certainly not," said Tuftenham; and off he went to the "Tag and Squeamish" to retail this pretty piece of gossip. Of course it did not come round to Charlie in this form, as it underwent

many more additions, modifications, and per-
versions before it reached him; but he ascertained pretty surely that the gentleman had
received his *coup de grâce*, and he was happier
for the intelligence. The robin and the frost
were to blame.

Most things went on quietly and consistently
at Brain Lees Manor House, the sacred grove
in which Captain Armstrong instructed British
youth in the mysteries of military science. He
continued pertinaciously his grog and rubber;
the Cantab regaled himself with a short pipe and
Burton beer when the day's cramming was over;
and the young disciples of the establishment
were as consistent in their habits of idleness,
duck-hunting, badger-baiting, and rat-catching,
as *the Duke* could possibly have desired. They
showed a wonderful energy in these matters.
Energy, we are all assured, on the word of an
eminent schoolmaster, is far above learning: but
a very keen-sighted friend of mine declares in
favour of *luck*.

One morning, however, on Charlie's return
from a visit at Gilsland, he found the house and
family in a terrible state of excitement. Craven

was missing. Had he gone by himself the loss might have been remedied ; but he had taken no less than Matilda, in her best bonnet, with him. By the time the Captain was awake to the fact, Miss Armstrong had become Mrs. Craven, and was already on her third sheet of repentance, unmixed at present with any regret. Of course he was furious ; all dram-drinkers are ill-tempered and excitable, and old Armstrong was no exception to the rule. He cursed his servants and his gods, his profession, his pupils, and his wife, whom he accused as the cause of his misfortunes, and then appealed to Charlie, and burst into tears. The lady was less affected. On a general review of the whole case, she drew a lively picture of a reconciled daughter-in-law, a reluctant but undoubted recognition of her claims by the aristocrats of the family, and an occasional entrance on to the threshold of good society through " My daughter, Mrs. Craven ; " whose son might possibly become Lord Doolittell, by not more than half-a-dozen unexpected deaths.

"Dear me, Captain Armstrong," said she, "don't make such a fool of yourself—she's old

enough to know her own mind; and he might
have done worse. Drat his uncle; who's he,
that he should give himself airs, I should like
to know?"

And so she carried her complaints about
among her neighbours, but applauded herself
at home.

Hypercriticism may ask what this has to do
with the business. I admit, nothing whatever.
Perhaps nothing more may be heard of Mr. or
Mrs. Craven during these volumes: but it was a
startling episode in the life of Charlie's, tutor,
and could scarcely be omitted. Besides, it has
its moral, to parents, tutors, and pupils.

We may as well make short work of them all.
Craven became an ensign, and took his wife to
India; for the uncle and the aristocratic family
were inexorable. He died after three years'
service, as others have done before him; and his
widow, the Widow Craven, who never forgot her
uncle, Lord Doolittell, though she reviled him
prettily during her husband's life, became Mrs.
Major O'Toole, of the Mounted Flybynights, and
led a miserable life, somewhat between that of a
vivandière and a camp-follower. Old Armstrong

had the pleasure of instructing several young O'Tooles in after years; and Mrs. Armstrong mended the little breeches of these brave little warriors, with many a sigh that they were not Cravens.

CHAPTER X.

STRONG OF THE STABLE.

"An honest man is able to speak for himself, when a knave
is not."—2 *Henry IV.*

CHARLIE THORNHILL had just finished, what in
racing language is politely called his last sweat,
and was lying in his room preparatory to another
attack upon those eternal logarithms, when a
knock at the door summoned him.

"Man below wants to see Mr. Thornhill," said
the servant.

"What's he like?" said Charlie, through the
door.

"Looks like an Irishman. I think he is one,
sir."

"Why so?" again demanded our hero.

"Talks like it, sir, and says he's so thirsty."

"Where does he come from; and what does
he want? Not a gentleman, is he?"

"Oh! no, sir. Won't give no name; and says

he can't leave the house till he's seen Mr. Thornhill."

" Well, then, take care of the hats and coats, and I'll be down in five or ten minutes. I dare say he wants money."

" Most on 'em do, sir. I'll tell him to wait in the hall."

Charlie rose, completed a rapid toilette, and descended. There was no one in the study, and thither he conducted his client. "I think you want to speak to me; my name's Thornhill."

The man did not answer immediately, and Charlie had time to run him over. He was evidently from the Sister Isle: it did not require him to talk to recognise that fact. He had a quantity of shaggy brown hair, a thick beard, with which his eyes and the general colour of his face were at variance. High cheek-bones and ferret-looking eyes gave a character of cunning to him. His dress was peculiar. He twisted a low-crowned hat in his hand. His clothes were well made, but very shabby. A shepherd's plaid shooting-coat and waistcoat; a scarlet woollen neckcloth, with the ends hanging down ; and a pair of brown trousers, very tight, and terminating in three buttons over the rough and thick highlows he wore, completed the suit. What was he ?   A helper; a wandering conjuror; a pedestrian attendant on a pack of hounds; or a Newmarket tout out of season ?   The bird of Jove is said to be rapid of flight; but before he could have swooped the depth of a moderate house, Charlie's mind had taken in thus much.

"Now then, what is it, my man ?   Where do you come from ? "

" I come to-day from Mr. Downy's."   Oh! oh! thought Charlie, something wrong about Œdipus. Now I suppose he wants to see my brother.

"Are you engaged in the stable ?"

"No, sir; not exactly."   One of those rascally touts, thought Charlie.   It's about time honest men cut the turf.   And indeed the gentleman was right.

"Well, then, you know something about our horses.   Now, out with it like a man.   Let's hear what the information's worth, and you shall have it."

"Faix, then, your honour's right: it is about the horses."

" Which of them ? " said Charlie.

"Well, it's not Kathleen, nor the two-year-old; them's all right : and I seen Jonathan Wild the day before yesterday. Och! he's the picture;" during which speech the man continued to turn and twist the rim of his hat, which might have been better, to have stood the wear and tear. "But there's a big brown horse, your honour knows, as isn't quite clane-bred ; and—and—he's more of a steeple-racer, or whatever your honour calls 'em."

"Œdipus, you mean ; the horse that's engaged in a match ? "

"Well, Captain, I wouldn't engage for the name," said the Irishman. "I don't well know about them foreigners, but that's the horse that I mane."

"Is there anything amiss with him ? " said Charlie, rather nervously, for he knew how heavily Tom had backed him. "The horse was all right a week ago." Here Charlie looked closely at the man, and a sudden idea that he was not unknown to him set him thinking where he could have seen him.

" He's right enough now, and will be so, maybe, this week or two, or whenever the match is; but he won't be right the day before, nor the day itself. But I see your honour don't belave me."

"If what you tell me is true, you've some object in telling me," said Charlie, who was still endeavouring to recall the place in which he had seen his companion.

"'Deed, I have, then. It's to save yer money, and, maybe, yer horse; but I'll be murther'd if it's known that I told yer honour anything about it."

"You haven't told me anything about it yet. What is it you fear?"

"What is it I fear? I fear I'll be murther'd," said Pat, taking thought for himself.

"No, no; I mean for the horse," said Charlie, not so particular about an Irishman more or less in the world.

"For the horse? Sure it's poison."

"What makes you think there's any danger of that? Do you know the trainer, Sam Downy?"

"Do I know Sam Downy? 'Deed do I. He's done a queer thing or two, but he won't do that: he's right enough. It's the boys."

"Then why didn't you go to him at once?'

"He's a good man, is Sam Downy; but he's not a real gentleman, Misther Thornhill: he hasn't the blood in him. Wouldn't he think I'd be lying to him; with his own boys, and all? But it's true as gospel; and ye'll belave it, if ye lave the poor beast there till ye see." This seemed a very conclusive condition, but Charlie was too English to enter into it. So he said again—

"This may be true; but I can't test it. How do you know this?"

"Faith, I do know it. I heard it."

"Men hear more lies than truth in this world."

"Your honour's right this time. So your honour will send for the horse away?"

But Charlie was too stanch to his point to be shaken off like this, so he said again—

"Not unless you give me your authority. I won't move a hand or foot in it unless you do. Take your news to Mr. Downy."

"You won't? Then, sir, by Jakers, it's just George is my authority; divil a soul else." This was said with a sort of obstinate energy, which impressed Charlie somewhat with its truth.

"And what did George, as you call him, tell you?"

"Just nothing at all. What for would he tell me? Faith it was the lad as looks after the horse, as he told it to. Says he, 'Tim,' says he, 'it must be done. Look at that. That's your own.' And he brings out a beautiful English note, and spreads it out. 'And you'll have a handsome trifle put on for ye besides, now the party knows which way it's to be.' And the boy said something about the Squire, maning your brother, and how he loved the horse. And then the blackguard promised that he wouldn't hurt him, only make him safe. And he's to have a key the night before the race; and if the money given for it is anything, it 'll be a golden key that unlocks the stable-door."

"And where were you when you heard all this?" said Charlie.

"Wasn't I asleep in an outhouse, and they two was talking to one another all the time about Mr. Thornhill's horse."

"And what George is this, that you seem to know so much about?"

"He's George Ritsom; I knew him when I

first see him : for we were together, maybe,
fourteen or fifteen years ago.   He was always a
bad 'un, was George.   They do say as he's groom
to a gentleman—Misther Graves, they call him,
a great sporting gentleman."   This threw a new
light on the subject, and made Charlie pause
before he rejected such doubtful evidence.   He
knew Wilson Graves; he knew his character;
and he knew that, for some inexplicable reason,
he had been laying against the horse, by commission, up to the very day.

"And your object is to serve me ?"

"It is."

"And how have I deserved that at your
hands ?" said Charlie, who, being one of those
men who acted upon some sort of principle himself, expected others to do the same.

The Irishman looked down, with a foolish
look, as though not understanding the question.
At length he raised his head, and ignoring the
previous question, he said, " Then ye'll look
afther your brother's horse, sir ; I'll go bail he'll
pay ye for the throuble : I never saw a finer
beast.   He's a grand horse altogether."

" Listen to me, and never mind about the

horse. I want to know what I ever did to or for
you that you should be anxious to serve me.
You must have a reason." As Charlie spoke he
rose from his chair, and placed his back, apparently with no purpose, against the door. The
movement was not lost on the Irishman, who
looked nervous, and again resorted to a vacant
stare, whilst he appeared to con the last question.

"What ye ever did to me? Sorrow a thing
ye ever did to me. Maybe ye'll mind the puppy
ye lost——"

"And got back again. My good man, I'm not
likely to forget it in a hurry. Did you hold my
horse at Tattersall's that morning?"

"Well then, your honour, I won't decave you.
You're too quick for the likes o' me, anyhow.
How'll the dog be? I heard that ye had her
back."

"She's up-stairs at this minute, and well. But
why did you come here to me to-day?"

"Would I make a scandal and a talking in a
gentleman's stable? and, maybe, he know it all
the while, and——"

"What's that, you scoundrel?" said Charlie,
interrupting him; "you dare to insinuate that my

brother knows of such a thing, or ever heard of such a thing, for one minute, and connived at it. It's a lucky thing for you he didn't hear you say it. I believe he'd have wrung your neck on the spot. He's quicker tempered than I." And here Charlie smiled grimly; for he knew the laxity of stable morality to take too seriously what the Irishman might have considered part of the business of turf-management.

" Och, yer honour, is it him ye calls the young Squire ? Would I mane such a thing of a gentleman like that ? It's Misther Downy, sure, I was thinking of. Ye see, your honour, I've been a bit in the horse line myself, and, though I'm out of luck, I know a trifle about them sort. They're not the same as a gentleman-born." And Mike, for it was he, began to feel quite comfortable at having put Charlie off the scent as to the motives of his information. He was wise enough to hold his tongue, a thing few people can do just in the right place; there's many a good cause spoilt by over-talking. At length Charles Thornhill looked at him steadily and said, " Supposing this information to be true —and I shall take care to see whether it is or no

—what is the price? You haven't travelled with it here for nothing. What do you want?" And Charlie resumed his seat by the fire.

Mike stared for a moment, and then drawing up with a certain dignity, which assorted badly with his tight brown trousers and highlows, said, "Faith, it's no fault of your honour's that ye can't understand me. I was better off once, and I'd a good name to the back of me; but it's a long time ago. I haven't a rag on me now that wasn't given to me; and it's not proud that I'd be, under the circumstances, of the name I'd get if I'd my deserts. But I'd rather walk barefooted to the next jail, or, what's harder fare, to the parish workhouse, than I'd rob one of your name for doing an honest action." Mike burst into tears, the first he had shed for many a long year; and before Charlie had recovered from his astonishment, he was out of the garden-door, and into the road, on his way back again.

No sooner was he gone, which Charlie ascertained beyond all doubt, by looking after him out of the gate, than he began pondering on the strange occurrence. It was not odd that a man should wish to tamper with a horse in training:

such things had happened before. But it was odd that the man who did so had no more sense of shame or obligation than appeared to be the case with Wilson Graves. What, too, brought Mike there to tell him? He looked like a scoundrel; doubtless he was one (for appearances are not always deceitful); and yet the man takes a journey and refuses money, two things that none but a madman would be guilty of, instead of participating in the robbery, as he might have done. All that struck Charlie as singular, to say the least of it. He liked getting to the bottom of a thing. He knew there was a motive for every action, and he had that sort of determination which likes to test it. Now, he was as far off as ever. However, here was a fact—the man had been to him, and had asserted such and such things, leaving him to deal with them.

Charlie's doubts resolved themselves finally into three distinct propositions. When once that happens with a man of his character we may look for a speedy solution of difficulties. For, if not over sharp, he was exceedingly honest; and a sort of useful common sense assisted a conscientious view of right and wrong. His first impulse was to take the matter in hand himself; but a moment's reflection showed him that that had its objections, the simplest of which was that he had no sort of authority whatever to do so. The horse was not his; the stables were not his; the money was not his. He possessed nothing but the information. Should he go at once to Tom? After all, he was the person most concerned. But prudence told him, that if it could be disproved, he might as well spare Tom some very uncomfortable sensations, the impulses of that gentleman rather tending to jump to conclusions and act upon them with a very liberal allowance of energy. Charlie was loth to believe that Wilson Graves was concerned in such a nefarious business; still, appearances were against him. Should he see Mr. Samuel Downy? The only real objection to this was the recollection that he had not secured the cooperation, nor even the address, of his informant, and the injustice he might be doing an innocent boy. Still it was eminently Downy's business to know it, and to fathom it; and if he knew it already, as the Irishman had hinted, the sooner his employers knew it the better for the interests of the turf. There was the journey down, which took up time, a very valuable part of Charlie's capital: strange to say, he spared it grudgingly. One cigar, and a turn in the garden, settled his deliberations in favour of the last course. He put it into practice at once.

Mr. Samuel Downy was one of the stars of his profession; and, as he had risen to its heights from its lowest depths, through all the gradations, he fully comprehended its details. He had that grand virtue, that whilst he was in dignity of carriage, and redness of face, the superintendent of his establishment, he was not above descending to the minutiæ of his own stable-boys. It was the making of him, as it has been of the great Duke and some other remarkable persons. Sensual indulgence unhappily produced gout, and gout infirmity; otherwise Mr. Downy would have been an active man; as it was, he was a very clever one. He was placed in a situation of much temptation, which he resisted so successfully as never to have been found out. He might have had a brother-in-law who laid against the favourite in Sam Downy's stable, whilst his owner continued to back him, and his trainer to prog-

nosticate certain victory; but he took very good
care that it was not known if such were the case.
The public took him by the hand, and put him
on a pedestal, from which a fall would have
shaken him sorely.

"Now, my dear Downy, take another piece of
buttered toast, and don't vex yourself about the
Captain's horse; he'll be all right in the morning,
I dessay," said Mrs. Downy, one evening, as she
poured out the master's cup of tea with one hand
and stroked the flaxen curls of a young Downy
with the other.   But the master's soul was not
to be subdued by buttered toast on this occasion,
for the second favourite for the next year's two
thousand guineas had hit his leg in his gallop,
and was decidedly lame.

"Oh! yes; I know he'll be all right again,"
replied Downy, a little mollified by the attention;
"but lor! how they will knock him about if the
touts get sight of him; and there's lots of 'em
about, Sally; so I tell ye. Why, he'll be knocked
clean out of the betting."

"Well, then, you go and knock him clean in
again. Now then, Jim Turner, what do you
want lurking about here after the stables is done

up? If you're come after Bessy Knowles, she's gone home to her friends, so you may go after her." You see Mrs. Downy had not yet risen to the high social position she afterwards occupied. She married Sam, when he was a poor man, several years back; and she had not yet accomplished those company manners which belong to the wives of our topping trainers. Indeed, she never did quite reach that pinnacle of perfection which some have attained; but she was a good honest woman, a great favourite with the gentlemen, and wore a cap which resembled a triple crown in a harlequin jacket.

"I don't want none o' your Bessy Knowleses," said the boy, laughing. "I wants the master."

"Well, out with it then: what have you got to say to the master? here he is."

"No, no, Mrs. Downy, thank ye; I'll see Jim after tea in my room; you go and wait for me in the kitchen, Jim. My dear, send little Sally there to fetch my slippers: blest if I don't think I got a little touch o' my old friend coming." Saying which, Mr. Downy nursed his leg, and Jim Turner retired to the kitchen to make love to Bessy Knowles's substitute.

It was about nine o'clock at night: the low, snug room which Mr. Downy called his own, and in which he smoked his evening pipe, and drank his evening glass, was warm and well lighted. Both Mr. and Mrs. Downy were well satisfied with its comforts. It presented to their eyes something brighter than wit, and warmer than friendship. Downy smoked in silence, and Mrs. Downy did the talking at intervals. But her lord and master was more than usually mysterious. Jim Turner had long been dismissed; and the new cook had washed up, and was reposing in front of the kitchen fire, when they were startled by the bayings and barkings of all the dogs, and a loudish ring at the bell. There is much character in that single action. The present tintamar seemed to say, "I'm coming in whether you like it or no;" so Mrs. Downy put a cheerful countenance upon it, and after wondering whether it was some half-dozen people, who were not likely to come, attended to a second appeal, by snatching up a candle, with "Lor love the man, he's in a hurry, whoever he is," and going to the door.

"How do, Mrs. Downy?" said Charlie, as

soon as he got inside; "how's Mr. Downy. I hope I haven't disturbed you; but it's rather late to come down without writing. However, I want to have five minutes' conversation with Downy, if he's up;" and here, having been subjected to Mrs. Downy's scrutiny, she recognised the speaker.

Of the two brothers, Downy perhaps rather preferred the younger. Tom hurried him; was too impetuous altogether; would back his own prejudices; and contradicted him unmercifully. Charlie spoke little to him; was monosyllabic in his remarks; and kept up accidentally that feeling of mysticism so grateful to the heart of a trainer, or a turfite. He was greatly relieved to see Charles Thornhill in illustration of Mrs. Downy's remark as she opened the door: "Bless me, my dear, if here ain't Mr. Thornhill; who'd a' thought it at this time o' night?"

She took an early opportunity of setting the tower of Babel in the harlequin jacket aright, and then proceeded at once to ring for another glass, more hot water, and what Irishmen know as the "materials." Charlie was not averse to the arrangement; mixed himself a tumbler of

whiskey and water, and accepted a cigar, which
had been a present from his brother to Sam
Downy.

In the mouth of an orator language is very
uncertain in its mode of operation. It takes a
long time to make a man understand anything.
But Charlie was no orator; so that he was not
long in making Sam Downy understand the exact
state of his suspicions as regarded Œdipus. As
Charles Thornhill progressed with his story,
he might naturally have expected some remark,
some affirmative or negative grunt. Not a
sound relieved or assisted him. Slowly and
methodically Sam Downy puffed away at his
pipe; and as the relater approached the crisis,
nothing but a little more prolonged expul-
sion of smoke betrayed an increased interest
in the story. He finished; and Sam puffed
away and looked steadily into vacancy. At
length stopping his pipe with his little finger,
and taking a gulp at his whiskey and water, he
turned slowly round to Charlie, and said—

"Oh! that's the game is it? Do you believe
it?"

"I can scarcely say that I do. I haven't told

my brother, but I thought it right to come here."
Charlie had been so reassured by the trainer's
coolness, that he really now very much doubted
the truth of the story, whatever he might have
done. After another half minute, collecting himself by an effort, he replied to the question—
"No! I do not believe it."

"I do!" said Sam, emitting a cloud of smoke
which spoke volumes.

"Any reason?"

"Half a dozen." Here Charlie waited for one
of these half-dozen reasons; but he was doomed
to disappointment, for Downy continued to smoke
in silence, and then "he drank and smoked, and
smoked and drank, and smoked again." Charlie
was too prudent to interrupt his meditations
with rash inquiries. After, however, a considerable pause in the conversation he ventured to
ask—

"What sort of a boy is it that looks after the
horse?"

"Very good boy; good as most, better than
most."

"Do you suspect him then?"

"Yes."

"Why?"

"Because he's a liar and a coward. They go together."

"Then is that your idea of a good boy, better than common, Downy? What an experience of youth yours is!"

"There's only one out of ten that wouldn't be too bad for the Old Bailey if you could know half the truth. The boy's been lying to me lately about a key, and his being out at night. I've had an eye on him; the horse is all right, and you'll say to-morrow it's all over but shouting."

"If we can circumvent this rascal George, whoever he may be." Charlie turned his cigar in his mouth, looked at it attentively without seeing it, and went on—"But how to do that?"

"Leave it to me. I shall write to Mr. Thornhill to-morrow, sir; and if he'll put me on sixty pounds to forty, I shall be much obliged to him. I'll guarantee him all he's laid upon the horse against anything wrong now."

"Well, then, good night, Downy. I'll be with you to-morrow about nine." And Charlie walked off to the Stapleford Arms.

"Now, Sally, let's have that rasher in directly.
I begin to feel a bit peckish." Mr. Downy still
dined early.

The next morning dark clouds lowered
omniously above; and there had evidently fallen
much rain in the night. Charlie was punctual
to his appointment.

"That's a nice colt the one we've passed," said
Charlie; "good useful legs and feet, and big
thighs and hocks."

"Orlando and Durandarté," replied Mr.
Downy; "great turn o' speed." This was said
almost in a whisper.

"Strip that Oaks filly, Ned." And the boy,
slipped off the clothing. "That's a nice filly,
Mr. Thornhill;" and he ran his hand approv-
ingly over the mare's quarters. "Quiet!" added
he, as she lashed out with one leg; "quiet can't,
ye? This way, sir."

Charlie turned from his inspection into a dark
doorway, and Mr. Downy putting a key into the
lock, turned it, and they were in the presence of
Œdipus. "Now, where's Jim Turner?"

"Here, sir," said a good-humoured looking
youngster about eighteen or nineteen; not very

strong-minded to all appearance, and mischievous, but not malicious.

" How's the horse ? "

" All right, sir." Jim stripped him in a minute, and wiped him down with an old piece of silk handkerchief. The trio stood and surveyed him. He was a good-looking horse; and his appearance told no falsehood. His coat had been singed down closely, but looked glossy and well. He was a long, low horse, able to carry about 13 st.; and though, as Mike had said, he was not a " clane-bred 'un," still he looked it all over. He had a fine, intelligent head, not too small, well set on to a rather muscular neck, which required no steadying from adventitious aids. His shoulders were beautifully laid, but a little thick and weight-carrying to a fastidious eye. Good legs and arms in the proper place ; and hardy of feel and appearance. Behind the saddle he was beautiful; and his length from the hips was very great. His hocks were well let down, and under him; and with the exception of the blemish from which he took his name, he appeared to be almost faultless. His perform- ance over a country was as perfect as his symmetry; and he required nothing but skilful steering to render victory pretty certain.

"Is William ready with old Saucebox to lead ?"

" Yes, sir," said Jim.

"Then on with the cloths directly; you shall see him gallop, sir." And Charlie saw the horse walk and gallop; and he never saw him look or go better. So he wrote a letter to his brother as soon as he reached Armstrong's, telling him of his journey, its object, and satisfactory termination; and he trusted to old Downy's sagacity to defeat any plots, if any existed, fully confident that the man was as honest as it was possible to be, living in an atmosphere of so much temptation.

CHAPTER XI.

MERCANTILE.

"Faber quisque fortunæ suæ."

I HAVE given the lovers of horseflesh a good turn lately: I should like to go back to commercial life. *Toujours perdrix* is not so well. Besides, I shall be suspected of a *penchant* for sporting novel-writing, of all things to be avoided. Guide then, O Muse! my pen from the heroic strains of Pythian or Olympic gamès, and from the seductive charms of stable eloquence, to the less stable designs of commercial life. Let me repose a while from the exciting themes of love, intrigue, and robbery, on the eider-down pillow of mercantile respectability. Nor think shame of me, fashionable reader, if I am about to plunge my hero in scenes unknown to his progenitors, since the originator of that honoured name, the goldsmith and money-lender of Lombard Street, retired from the debts and disasters of the Merry

Monarch, and his swindling mates, to found a family at Thornhills. Who are the merchant princes, who are the millionaire stock-jobbers of merrie England ? They occupy the places of honour in great men's houses. A Plantagenet still has honour, too, when the twigs of the broom he bears are from the gardens of the Hesperides, tipped with gold.

For some days after his interview with Henry Thornhill, Roger Palmer was thoughtful, almost depressed even for him. But the funds went up, and he got better. That unfortunate allusion to his family affairs, and the bluntness of the banker, had set him thinking in the right direction. But a few weeks served to obliterate much of the impression. He had two unconquerable allies, which he called in to his assistance. His long-cherished resentment, which being the stronger feeling time strengthened instead of weakening ; and his sense of gratitude, which had better be called his love of money. The dead and almost forgotten Geoffrey Thornhill was ever alive to him as the benefactor of the house of Mint, Chalkstone, Palmer, and Co. ; and of himself particularly. Norah, still alive, was dead to him ;

or remembered as one who would have lavished
his beloved gold, even to the last farthing, on a
gambler and a roué.   And had she not preferred
an empty-headed stranger, weak and unstable,
without a principle or a shilling, to a brother and
a man, strong, and consistent, with intellect,
reputation, and wealth ?   Norah was paying
dearly for her whistle.

He had made up his mind to do the greatest
amount of good to the Thornhill family at the
least present sacrifice of his own feelings.   An
obvious mode of relieving any man's pecuniary
necessities, or of conferring substantial benefit
upon him, is simple.   Pay into his bankers a
draft for 50,000*l*.   This is supposing you have
double the money and wish to share it with him.
This, however, requires one or two conditions to
make it feasible.   The man must be a needy,
dependent, shameless kind of person, to whom
you would give it ; unless some strong chain of
relationship or personal service bind him to its
acceptance.   Roger Palmer never contemplated
parting with such a comfort, any more than
Charlie Thornhill would have accepted it.   Roger
Palmer did not regard 50,000*l*. in hard cash as,

2500*l.* per annum; but as a sacred idol, which could only be parted with to the man who should stand in his shoes. The income derivable from it might be given up. It hardly assumed the appearance of a hand, a finger, or a nose of the idol. It was an essence derivable from that tutelary influence which seemed to be thrown off for the advantage of one worshipper, it is true; but the sacred figure remained intact to its possessor. But would Charlie Thornhill reject the essence? There was a difficulty in making the proposal, it is true. Roger Palmer was deficient neither in tact nor discernment; and though he knew little of the man, he knew enough of his character to doubt.

Banking, that is, prosperous banking, is a very pleasant amusement. The senior partner is usually a dignitary, a baronet (if not of James I.'s creation), an M.P., and a most influential authority on all matters, in and out of the house, connected with finance. So it was with the firm of Mint, Chalkstone, and Palmer. Sir Julep Mint was a very great man. If he had not been a banker he would have been Lord Mayor. He had the seeds of greatness in

him. He was married to a lady in her own
right, and was called Lord Soapstone from the
name of his place and the dignity of his manners.
In a word, he was a pompous ass, and a very
low churchman. Chalkstone was a much better
fellow all over. He was a good hard liver; ate
a dinner every day of his life, and if he ever had
the gout, had earned it. He drove off his enemy
by horse exercise. Was not a bad man over a
country, and kept half-a-dozen first-class weight-
carriers in the roothings of Essex; certainly the
best provincial country in England, and not far
short of the shires. He was an easy man to deal
with. For though he said it in a blunt manner,
he usually said what he meant.

In a large, comfortably furnished room, at the
back of the *comptoir*, and connected with it by
large and handsome glass folding-doors, one
morning in December sat the three partners,
active partners, of the respectable firm above
alluded to. They had under consideration the
feasibility of taking into partnership some
younger man, who would put a certain capital
into the business, and work gratuitously for a
certain number of years, until the seed he had

sown should produce an abundant harvest. There were plenty of such young men to be found; but there were not so many thirty thousand pound notes to be met with, and somehow or other, banking was not in its zenith. There had been a tremendous smash or two, especially among the low-church party, and it required time to give the public confidence. Again, Sir Julep had lots of daughters, but no son, not even a son-in-law. Those who were high enough to aspire to that happiness were too worldly, the rest were nowhere. Chalkstone was without children, and had a Caligula-like fancy for making his bay horse a partner. He often declared that he was the only one of his acquaintance that he could trust. I wonder whether Caius Cæsar or old Boots had an equally sufficient reason for appointing to the consulship! Be that as it may, the two seniors being failures, the appointment fell to Roger Palmer. Much to the astonishment of his colleagues, he accepted the onus, guaranteeing the money, and only asking two or three days for some necessary correspondence. So reasonable a request could not be gainsaid. Due respect

was had for the superior age and intelligence of
the junior partner of the firm.   Whilst he lived
it was founded upon a rock; might his successor
be like him?

"You propose to send him abroad to conduct
the foreign business first, Mr. Palmer; it's a
great responsibility."

"Rather, Sir Julep, as a representative of our
house; he must be a gentleman, if possible, of
some position."

"Most undoubtedly, most undoubtedly; we
are in your hands, my good sir, and it must be
evident to our foreign correspondents that we
can send out no counterfeit, no counterfeit in
any sense.   It behoves the aristocracy, in times
of danger, like the present ——"

Here Chalkstone, in anticipation of a speech,
interrupted the worthy baronet: "Let's have a
good fellow, Palmer, into the kennels, into the
bank, I mean.   Fresh blood, sir, is a grand thing
in a pack of hounds—body of directors I should
say; and I hardly know any kennel we could fall
back upon, with any better chance of success,
than our friend Palmer.   A good, steady, true,
old-fashioned, line-hunting, that is, an honest.

intelligent, gentlemanly, young man, possessing the requisite amount of industry and pluck, and —and——"

"Money," added Roger Palmer, with a little sigh, for he couldn't help feeling it, though he had made up his mind with the heroism of a Spartan.

"Are you going my way?" said Sir Julep, with one of his most polished and condescending bows; "my brougham is at the bottom of the street; I'm on my way to the lying-in hospital; it's the anniversary of the Dorcas Society, and the little help that Lady Elfrida can afford we are only too happy to bestow: I can put you down, and go on for her."

"Or come with me, Palmer, my cab's at the door, and I should like you to see my new brown horse. I know you like a horse, although you pretend not to;" and Chalkstone almost pushed him out of the room before him.

"No, Sir Julep, thank you; no, no, Chalkstone; I can't afford to have my neck broken before this business is settled, you know. Let me walk home. It is but a step. I shall let you know, in a day or two, all about my nominee. The money's right enough; the money's right; and that's the great consideration;" and away went the little ‘miser, as quickly, and as jauntily, as if he had been a treasury clerk of five-and-twenty, with four hundred a-year. He knew that walking by yourself was cheaper than riding with other men.

The result of this conversation was a letter to Charles Thornhill. It reached him at a time when circumstances made it more acceptable than usual. Charlie's military ardour had never been great. He had never been attacked with scarlet fever, or at so early an age that it left no traces behind it. It was the turning-point of his life. All men have the turn; but few know it, and many neglect it. Verily, industry is a great thing, learning is a great thing, energy is a great thing, but *luck* is the greatest.

CHAPTER XII.

A FIRST VISIT.

"Utere convivis, non tristibus utere amicis."

THERE was a frost at Melton—indeed in most places. In vain the after-dinner zealots kicked the heels of their boots into the ground; in vain they looked at the thermometer; in vain they inquired after the moon. The frost would not go, so they did. Some to London; some to shooting quarters; some to agreeable country houses. The horses remained in Melton, to wake rude echoes from the hard roads as they passed to morning exercise, slipping and sliding, here, there, and everywhere; their riders loading the morning air with the thin clouds of their tobacco; the masters lounging in bed, and impatient at the weather which made them thus inactive.

"When are you going, Thornhill? This is the third day, and it looks like lasting. Everybody, except you and me, is gone to town. They were all off yesterday. Tailby skated to cover, and waited till one o'clock, but the horses could hardly trot, so we came home again. I'm told the Oakley haven't been stopped at all."

"Very likely not, but I shan't go to see : I'm off to-day," replied Tom Thornhill, but he did not think it necessary to add "*where*." Either it was not sufficiently important, or far too important, to be mentioned. The assumption was that he was bound to London; the fact was that his road lay to Gilsland. He was not a man to make himself unhappy about a frost; and the Dacres' invitation, which had been accepted conditionally, was regarded now as the greatest boon.

So Thornhill ordered his valet, and his valet ordered the post-horses; and having sent over a groom with a couple of hacks to the Dacre Arms, and having left orders for the stud to be forwarded in the event of a sudden thaw, he himself started about four o'clock for Gilsland.

The house was not full, but there was a good sprinkling of men and two or three women. A dowager to assist Mrs. Dacre in her hospitalities, or schemes; and a dear friend or two of the girls, without which no young woman of well-regulated mind seems capable of going through life. They write an infinity of letters, have always a breakfast confidence though they may have slept together, and wear the same coloured neck-ribbons.

It is but fair to say that Alice had fewer weaknesses of this kind than most girls. Her nature was eminently affectionate, warm-hearted, and impulsive, but non-sympathetic. She was superlatively true. She had certain notions of right and wrong, of the fit and unfit, which she might have broken through under some circumstances, but not where her own interests were concerned. In the choice of an intimate she would have deceived neither herself nor another. This prevented close alliances with persons of her own sex and age. Besides which, she believed her mother and sister to be her truest friends, and most worthy of her confidences. She would have loved with heart and soul, possibly an unworthy object; but she would have done so with her eyes open, and would have died in an endeavour to stifle her love.

Edith Dacre was less qualified to fight against

that interesting partner of unmarried life, a
" dearest friend." She was more inclined to lean
upon somebody. Her character wanted support.
She was moderate enough in her demands; but
she did the letter writing and the matutinal confidence part of the business admirably. It is
but justice, however, to say that she had a limit
to her amicitial relations, and had mentioned not
even the name of Charles Thornhill nor Robinson
Brown to Lady Lucy Trevanon, the supposed
friend of her bosom, the depositary of blighted
affections and of rejected addresses.

Tom Thornhill was in time for dinner. He
stayed many days; and as he was in love when
he got to Gilsland, and had had the symptoms
on him ever since the end of last season, it is
not singular that the malady should have broken
out upon him in full force during the frost,
which lasted more conveniently for him than
for foxhunting.

The life in an English country house is much
the same everywhere. There was shooting for
the men; an occasional day with the rabbits,
and one or two grand battues. The covers at
Gilsland, though not rivalling those of Lord

——, were good enough. Mr. Dacre was not likely to be sent for by a committee of the House to give evidence on a new Poaching Bill, or to offer suggestions on the cause of the increase of crime, as, connected with overstocked preserves; but he had always his regular days during the season, and a frost at midwinter was too good an opportunity to be passed by.

Thornhill was an excellent shot. He was an excellent sportsman, which is widely different from a mere gunner. Whether he walked over the turnips and stubbles, whether he accompanied Harry Stapleton and the keeper to the common at the end of the park, or whether he was posted at the warmest corner of the cover to make slaughter of the thickest bouquet, he won golden opinions. All the men in the house talked of him. The ladies'-maids heard all about him. He was referred to and deferred to daily at the table, when questions arose amongst the men, and it is not extraordinary that the women caught the epidemic.

There was no hunting, it is true; but the less chance there appeared of a recommencement of that sport, so much the more did the conver-

sation turn upon it, as if, in very defiance of the
season, something was to be done. And here
Thornhill certainly was no mean authority·
What had *he* done with his horses ? What did
he think of the run from Loseby ? Was it
as good as Cheney said it was, and had he really
the best of it ? Yes, it was excellent, and Cheney
had far the best of it ; he, Thornhill, never
could get near him. His modesty disarmed the
foes which his courage might have made. The
women heard less of this, but they took their cue
from the men ; and Tom Thornhill was in the
ascendant.

Then they went to an election dinner. The
local papers reported Tom Thornhill's speeeh,
and all agreed that it was the most amusing,
if not the most erudite, of the evening. The
"Times" condescended to make an extract.
Eloquence always finds its way to the hearts
of the women. They skated, Thornhill admirably; and he insisted upon a sledge on the
ice for the ladies. They had some impromptu
charades ; he was the life and soul of the *corps
dramatique*. He was not much in the library,
but he seemed to be more or less *au courant* to

the literature of the day; thanks to the periodicals, which are supposed to do the heavy work, and which as effectually preclude the necessity of deep research as they quicken the taste for less meritorious productions.

Without wishing to hurt the feelings of my female readers, this is a character which seldom fails to awaken their interests; more especially when joined to a handsome person and a good rent-roll.

Guests went and came. Still Tom Thornhill remained. He had promised himself and Mr. Dacre a week's hunting round Gilsland, and the latter would not be denied. "Mr. Thornhill must find it very stupid here," said Mrs. Dacre. Next week, to be sure, they expected Harry Stapleton back; the General was coming, Lord and Lady Dunningfield, and Baron Hartzstein; and the frost looked like going. So Tom stopped on, nothing loth; and sent for his horses; and the frost did go, which is not usually the case when you send for your horses; and the guests came, which is not usually the case when you particularly want them; and everything was *couleur de rose.*

Meanwhile the Dunce of the family was making up for lost time. He had put everything pretty straight at Downy's. He had told his brother all his suspicions, who poo-pooh'd them of course, and in his multifarious employments had almost forgotten the subject. He had made up his mind to get through his examination, if it depended upon himself; and he felt inclined to believe old Armstrong when he said so. At least it was clear that no great amount of assistance was to be looked for from that learned pundit; and the young Cantab was so desperately afraid of Charlie that it was difficult to get out of him what he did know. Charlie Thornhill was not one to give up a thing he had once taken in hand: so he worked away every morning, indulging in a walk during the frost every afternoon, and pulling out of his pockets, at intervals, the dates of the Stuarts, the battles of the Wars of the Roses, George the Third's Ministers, the men of letters of Queen Anne's reign, a list of the British dependencies, the principal ports in Ireland, and the military stations of Hindostan, together with a long list of heterogeneous information, to the copying of which the Captain's abilities were limited. And yet there were several fellows got through in spite of the Captain, and made very good soldiers. What clever fellows they must have been!

One thing, in the middle of it all, Charlie did not do. He did not go so frequently to Gilsland. Since he heard of Robinson Brown's discomfiture he felt it would be bad for him. If it be possible to analyse his feelings at this time, perhaps, summed up in his own language, they may have amounted to this—" Only let me get over this examination, and the steeple-chace, and then we'll see all about it." The three together were too much for his simple soul.

" You had a good run to-day, Mr. Thornhill?"

" Not at all, Miss Dacre; what made you think so?" said Tom, lounging into the hall in scarlet, covered with the mud which accumulates on a thaw, and desiring his servant to be sent to him.

" You look so happy; and I concluded it was the run," said Alice.

" One can scarcely be unhappy here: but I'm not so wedded to horse and hound as you

imagine. It really pains me to think that I can
be so far misjudged." At the same time Tom
looked brighter than ever, and not at all pained.

"Misjudged? Oh! Mr. Thornhill. No one
misjudges you; but——" Here Alice felt the
colour beginning to rise. Tom waited for the
fruit of the "but." "But, but, with all your
love of—of—of——" (Alice would like to have
said "play") "hunting and racing, it is odd that
you should find much pleasure in our quiet
home." Here she thought she had said too
much, so she added: "Unfortunately, my brother
is gone to Berne; but the General comes to-
morrow, with Lord and Lady Dunningfield, and
then you will be better amused."

Here Thornhill's servant crossed the hall with
clothes, hot water, &c., &c., and it was necessary
to say something. "Martinet, Martinet. Oh!
he comes to-morrow," said he, in a quick, un-
meaning sort of tone. "Oh! ah! well! yes!
Capital fellow, Martinet. You know him well,
Miss Dacre, of course? He'll talk of nothing
but horses. He's forgotten the army almost.
Just recollects one circumstance; and then he
had a horse shot under him."

"No; I never saw him. This is his first visit here." Alice might have added, that he was asked especially to meet Thornhill as a racing ally. Mrs. Dacre thought he ought to be made as comfortable as possible. Martinet, Hartzstein, and Dunningfield, were all racing men; Stapleton did everything; and George Fitzgerald could show him the way to cover, and from cover, and discuss the run when they smoked their cigars at night. Mrs. Dacre was a very clever woman, and kept her own counsel. Martinet was delighted, Fitzgerald was flattered, and, excepting herself, I don't think any living soul had the slightest suspicion of her game. She hardly knew it herself, her skill was so ladylike, so profound.

"Lady Lucy Trevanon wants to know what became of Robinson Brown to-day, after they found. He was riding close by you, Thornhill, when Miss Edith Dacre and Lady Lucy arrived, and he wasn't seen afterwards."

Edith coloured, and looked hard at Lady Lucy, who was bent upon amusing herself at somebody's expense.

"Surely it's not *you*, Mr. Thornhill, that the

Heir Apparent has to fear?" Here Lady Lucy's eyes sparkled with malicious pleasure, and she saw her dearest friend fidgeting on her chair. The fact is, that Lady Lucy had been behind the scenes just to that dangerous point when people begin to conjecture what there is further on. Had she been thoroughly trusted she might have held her tongue now, but would assuredly have told every one of her acquaintance at a proper opportunity under the strictest seal of secresy.

Thornhill, with more good-nature than truth, with some little inkling of the state of affairs, said: "Robinson Brown was riding the horse with which they tried Reluctance the other day, and didn't want to exhibit his capabilities in my immediate neighbourhood. But, Miss Dacre, you never hunt?" The last speech was Greek to the ladies, and shut up Lady Lucy Trevanon.

"Never," said Alice, with a rather determined but good-humoured face.

"That means never will."

"You read countenances well, Mr. Thornhill. Surely one sportswoman is enough for a small stud. Besides, we have had our warning."

"Ah! I beg your pardon for reminding you of
——" Here Tom stopped suddenly.

"We never need to be reminded of it: it is a
pleasure to remember our obligations to your
brother. He has become very intimate here
lately."

"So I hear. I envy him the leisure and the
distinction." Tom began to think almost that
Alice was in love with Charlie.

"As to leisure, he hasn't much: the distinction, if it is one, is well deserved. We owe him
two lives out of the three."

"Charlie's a good fellow, Miss Dacre: too
good to go out of the country. I can't understand why he should go," rejoined Tom.

"I think I can," said Alice; "but it is not
everybody that would understand your brother."

"Quixotic?"

"Not the least in the world: never was good
common sense so strongly exhibited: I love his
independent spirit. You see he has made a
confidante of me."

How like Lady Marston she is, thought Tom.
And so she was, but stronger. She had lived
less in the world, and was less a woman of it.

It was quite clear she was not in love with
Charlie.   Could that ridiculous story about
Robinson Brown, Edith Dacre, and his brother,
be true ?

The ladies left the table, Lady Dunningfield
leading.

" What's doing about your brown horse,
Tom ?" said Mr. Fitzgerald, who lost no time in
leading the conversation at his end of the table.
" The frost won't suit him."

" I really don't know. I shan't back him
any more. They lay even, and I have laid odds
on him."   Mr. Dacre was busy with a pear,
but he looked up, and mournfully, at his
guest.

" Who rides Œdipus, Thornhill ?   The General wants to know," said Lord Dunningfield.
The General was deaf, and sat with his hand
behind his ear.

" My brother Charlie, General.   He wants
some holding."

" And who rides the mare ?" asked the General, winking his over-hanging brows.

" The owner," shouted Dunningfield again.
" I saw him to-day on a first-class horse.   I

don't think he can ride him. Your brother is three stone in your favour, Thornhill."

" I think not. You don't do Robinson Brown justice. He rides very well, Dunningfield; and his mare is fast, and can stay."

" You want the odds," said Lord Dunningfield.

" Not a halfpenny. But ask Fitzgerald."

" It's true, my Lord. He can ride, if all goes right, very well. He went beautifully from Crick Gorse, one day early this season, on the mare. He can't ride a bad horse, like Charles Thornhill. Few men can. But——"

" So!" said Hartzstein, who was anxious to exhibit his knowledge of languages, three of which he spoke imperfectly, but upon all occasions. His passion was the turf, his *beau idéal* of a man of fashion an English sportsman, and his vocabulary a mixture of the Viennese *salons* and the British stable. " So-o-o. Ye-e-es. I remember me vell. Monseigneur le Prince de Cambridge got avay mit de leading hounds, and Robainson Brown stock to him, like a bricks. He took all the fences first, and Monseigneur était content de le suivre. Mais enfin, they arrive at a regular sticker. ' Donnerwetter!'

says Robainson Brown, 'dies geht nicht, dere is no hole, and my horse is a little battu.' But he is suddenly becomes dam polite, is Robainson Brown; so he says, 'J'aurai l'honneur de vous suivre, mon Prince, you shall go first; I shall follow after.'"

"Bravo! Baron. And what did Monseigneur do?"

"Oh! ah! he attrapait—a devil of a cropper. Dornhill, I shall lay you five—five to four—in—in—what shall it be?—little horses, what you call ponies?" But Thornhill had just been summoned from the room by a servant, and nobody accepted the liberal offer.

Baron Hartzstein was just one of those men who are received in England nobody knows why, excepting that he had plenty of money or credit, dressed well, was always in a good humour, had excellent manners, and made himself pre-eminently English. He was supposed to be an agent of the Prince de ——, from Vienna, and had the management of the prince's stud in this country. He had been eminently successful for a foreigner; laid the odds or took them with the same cordiality, generally a point or two more than the market. He was not quite accredited by the highest-class foreigners, but nobody seemed anxious to throw down the glove: and as he had a bowing acquaintance with good men of his own country, and nobody was willing or able to answer the question, "Who is Hartzstein?" he held his own pretty firmly here.

The conversation had become decidedly *horsey* at the Baron's end of the table; and as Dacre and some neighbouring country gentlemen were not in a position to enter upon the relative merits of certain fillies and colts for the next year's Derby, the host gracefully rose from the table, and the gentlemen adjourned to the drawing-room.

CHAPTER XIII.

MATCH-MAKING.

"Je propose." "Jouez, s'il vous plait."

Tom Thornhill was not in the drawing-room, nor in the billiard-room. There was attraction in both. He was at that moment in Mr. Dacre's morning-room, in an arm-chair, and standing before him was a tall, strong, black-whiskered individual, whom we have met before; Thornhill had not.

"I assure you it's true. Make what ye will of it." The speaker spoke brusquely, but not disrespectfully.

"I've heard something of this before," said Tom, shading his eyes, and looking at the man by the dim light of a single reading-lamp.

"Not from me. And I know none else that would tell you."

"Then you've an accomplice that you know nothing about. Tell me exactly how much you have to do with it. I've already given you my word."

"I had everything to do with it. When I heard the horse belonged to a Thornhill, I cried off. I won't betray my associates. I have given you your caution : make what use of it you will, sir. I see you believe me."

In truth it was the same story as Charlie had already told him, from a different quarter. Tom did believe something about it; but he lived in an atmosphere of suspicion. "Why do you tell me instead of plundering me?"

"That's neither here nor there. There are plenty to plunder you without me. But make your mind easy; the owner of Reluctance and Sam Downy have nothing to do with it: but you'll be done this turn if you don't keep a strong look out." Here the man straightened his coat and buttoned it, gave one turn to his hat, and prepared to retreat.

"Will you tell me your name?"

"Have you ever heard of one Kildonald?" said the man, sternly.

The name jarred strangely on Thornhill. He had heard it years ago. In a moment his sad

recall from Eton, his father's indulgences, and
early and mysterious death, rose before him, and
linked themselves with the name. Was this the
man? Impossible. This man was not ten
years older than himself: scarcely so much.
Kildonald had never been heard of for years:
occasionally his name was mentioned, in no measured language, as a defaulter and a rogue.
"Yes, I have heard the name," said Tom, after a
pause.

"That's a name I might have borne had I had
my deserts. But they bend the twig, and cast
the tree into the fire because it doesn't grow
straight."

"My good fellow," said Tom, "whatever you
have done, you mean me an essential service.
Give me a means of serving you. You have had
a journey." And Tom crumpled a note in his
hand as he rose towards him.

"Not a shilling," said the man fiercely, and,
turning on his heel, was gone before Tom could
recover sufficiently from his astonishment.

After sitting in gloomy silence for a quarter of
an hour, running over the best days of his boy-
hood, and making some sombre reflections on

his present career, his coming match, and his
Newmarket engagements, Tom rose, shook him-
self free from his cares, and sauntered towards
the drawing-room. A sight of Alice would cure
him. The room was deserted. What! so late?
Eleven o'clock? All the women gone to bed?
No! they are in the billiard-room: General
Martinet and George Fitzgerald playing a game.

"The General giving you a lesson, Fitz?"
said Tom, at the open door.

"Yes; it's not very dear: a pound a game.
We've just finished. The ladies are waiting for
you and Dunningfield."

"I can't play to-night." And for the first time
in his life Tom was proof against persuasion and
odds. He took a seat by Alice Dacre, who never
found him so agreeable. Tom Thornhill was a
charming rattle; but no one knew him who had
not seen him in a graver mood. Lady Lucy
Trevanon would have been quite satisfied with
him as he was. Alice Dacre would have given
her life to have made him something more.
Which was the true lover?

There was a smoking-room at Gilsland, to
which men retired after the ladies, and Dacre

(who never smoked), or any persons of antiquated notions about six hours' rest or eight hours' rest, were gone to bed. Here was whist, a little higher than in the drawing-room; here were books on the Leger compared; here were the racing *on dits* of the day sifted; and, above all, a considerable deal of handicapping and match-making for the next Meeting took place over cigars and hock and seltzer water.

Tom Thornhill had had a bad time of it. During his stay he had sat late, and played high, not with success. Hartzstein was always ready to play; Dunningfield and Martinet were not averse to making up a rubber. George Fitzgerald played at times: he was one of those men, too, who did not always pay. Carlingford had been down, too, and carried away a hundred or two with him. Now and then Tom looked his position in the face, and saw a very deep gulf in his once ample resources. But his lawyers had never failed him yet, and had not even talked of a mortgage. Still it had been a ruinous winter.

One night, within a day or two of his intended return to Melton, the usual party was assembled.

The room was not large, nor well furnished, but comfortable; with a good fire very habitable. The cards were packed, and the men had turned to the fire in arm-chairs for half an hour's chat before separating. The Baron and Lord Dunningfield were going in the morning; the General followed the next day; and Fitzgerald's groom had got the route. As usual, some discussion was on the *tapis* about the relative merits of certain horses; and each maintained his opinion with considerable obstinacy.

"Then let the General handicap them for the Spring Meeting," said Thornhill.

"What are they?" said the General, who was the best judge in England, and who, naturally a shrewd, clever man, had bent all his powers of observation to the turf. "What are the animals?"

"Thornhill's Humble Bee and Harry Stapleton's Beau, for five hundred; two hundred forfeit," roared Lord Dunningfield, who sat on the General's deaf side.

"What are they—three year olds? what have they done? Nobody ever heard of them before?" said the General, laughing, and blinking his

heavy brows good-humouredly. " What's yours,
Thornhill ? "

" A —— bad one, General," said Tom, in a
cheerful voice, as if he was rather proud of his
incapacities. " The Bee's a roarer."

" So are you. What about the Beau, Stapleton ? didn't he run Medora to a head in the
last October Meeting ? "

" No; Medora gave him a seven-pound beating.
They're both three-year olds. Thornhill's is a
very bad un, but he's the best of the two; he
gave Rapparee twenty-one pounds and a beating
in a trial. Ask the Baron."

" What do you say, Baron ? "

" Tous les deux sont screws ! " said Baron
Hartzstein, delighted at the opportunity of exhi-
biting his idiomatic English.

" Well, now for it then ? " said the General :
" there's nothing to be got out of either of you ;
there's my half-crown," at the same time he
placed one on the table, and began a mental cal-
culation, which might have embraced the value of
the two Americas instead of two race-horses.

" And there's mine," said Thornhill, at the
same time relighting his cigar, which had gone

out in the discussion. " Don't forget the Bee's a roarer."

"And there's mine," said Harry Stapleton, opening a bottle of seltzer water. " There's mine. Remember, seven pounds worse than Medora."

But the General was deep in meditation, and rubbing his forehead slowly, over his shaggy brows, paid no attention at all to these suggestions. " Eight stone seven—eight stone seven —yes—yes " (with great deliberation). " Mr. Thornhill's Humble Bee, what's he by ? "

"Lazy Boy, out of Industry's dam," roared Fitzgerald.

"Mr. Thornhill's Humble Bee shall carry— eight stone s-e-v-e-n, and Mr. Stapleton's The Beau—The Beau—wait a moment, shall carry eight stone—yes, eight stone ; the ditch mile, on the last day of the next meeting, for two hundred, half forfeit; that's quite enough, quite enough. See you first, Thornhill : show."

Tom Thornhill opened his hand; no money was in it.

" Come, Stapleton, let's see yours ; " and he opened it with a like result.

"No match then," said a chorus of voices, whilst the General swept the three half-crowns into his pocket. The conversation went on as before.

"Come, I'll tell you what you shall do then, as you want a match," said the General. "The Beau shall run Baron Hartzstein's bay filly Cantatrice, at even weights, for two hundred, half forfeit. Cantatrice was bred in France, wasn't she, Baron?"

"Gewiss, of course, certainly; so you allow seven pounds, of course."

"Oh, I'm in the hands of the General," said Stapleton, producing another half-crown, which General Martinet immediately covered, an example followed by Baron Hartzstein, coupled with a suggestion too.

"You know we think Cantatrice a very moderate animal in France."

"Do you? then by Jove you must have some pretty good ones behind the curtain. *We* call her a very smart filly on this side the water, Baron; she's been unlucky."

"The General puts it mildly," whispered Fitzgerald to Thornhill.

"Well, now then, General, what is it? Let's have a run for it."

"So you shall; you shall carry eight stone, and the Baron eight stone five. Two hundred pounds, half forfeit, next meeting; that's the way I put the allowance. Show."

The Baron opened his hand with a sinister smile, and it held money.

"Then it's a match," said Harry Stapleton, showing his own. And again the General swept in the half-crowns.

"I'll lay 500 to 400 on Cantatrice," said Tom Thornhill.

"I'll take that," said Lord Dunningfield; "again if you like."

"No, that'll do for me at present;" and Thornhill finished his sherry and water, and prepared to move off.

"Stay a moment. Haven't you anything you can match at the first meeting, Thornhill? What's that colt you bought at Hampton Court the summer before last?"

"Orlando and Fly-by-night; oh, yes, he can gallop, but he can't stay, you know. Half a mile is about his distance," said Tom; "he's only a

two-year old, and not very forward; however, try
your luck, General."

"Well then, Lord Dunningfield, can't you do
something with the Fly-by-night colt? That
filly that was third for something good at Salis-
bury."

"You mean Maid Marion; she was beat a
length by that young Touchstone horse of
Scott's. I can run her for half a mile; make
the weights right, General." Lord Dunningfield
laughed, and threw down his money; the other
two half-crowns followed.

Again the General was buried in profound
thought. He shut his eyes, rubbed his forehead,
rumpled his time-thinned locks, and looked at
the ceiling, which he could not see for the
smoke, and then spoke oracularly.

"Thornhill's colt shall carry seven stone
seven, and Lord Dunningfield's filly—she's a
three-year-old—eight stone eight; last half mile
of the Beacon Course; the last day of the Spring
Meeting. Thornhill holds money. How are
you, my lord? No! then it's no match, and the
half-crowns are Thornhill's. That's the best
handicap I've made to-night. And now let's go

to bed," said he, throwing his cigar into the fire. "I dont know what Dacre will think of all this."

The same idea occurred to Tom Thornhill. When he turned on one side of his pillow he saw Alice Dacre. He could not be indifferent to her. A thousand trifles had assured him he was not. He'd go and live at Thornhills, and make his mother happy, and take her home a daughter she could love. How the two women at Thornhills would rejoice. He saw their approving faces through half the night. And then he turned on his pillow, and saw Dacre of Gilsland, stern and sad, and he thought Alice was very like her father about the eyes and mouth. Would he give his child to a gambler?

CHAPTER XIV.

ANOTHER OFFER.

"I like thy counsel; well hast thou advised."
Two Gentlemen of Verona.

On the morning of the day on which Tom
Thornhill was to leave Gilsland, as good or ill
luck would have it, he walked into the library,
where he found Alice Dacre turning over the
pages of an old periodical. It was quite clear
she was not reading them. He was in most
things a person of impulse, and it was just possible, notwithstanding his feelings, that, but for
this accidental meeting, Tom would have left
unsaid what he had to say.

An ominous silence reigned for a minute or
two, when Tom Thornhill looked up from the
paper he was pretending to read, and said in a
low voice, "Alice."

"Mr. Thornhill."

"Excuse the abruptness of my address. It

must have been evident to you during the few weeks I have been here that my happiness, everything I have in life, is dependent upon you. If I have been unable to impress you with this I have indeed failed;" and here Tom took a passive hand in his, and proceeded in language which is always incoherent at the best of times, and when perfectly sincere, more incoherent than usual.

Alice regained possession of her hand, and rising to her full height, placed it for support on the back of a chair. A blush rose to her cheek, and a tear hung on her eyelashes; and if she ever looked perfectly lovely, it was now, as she answered a portion of his eloquent appeal.

"Have I, indeed ? Have I led you to suppose that you were not indifferent to me ? "

" Forgive me if I have hurt you by what I have said. I was foolish, and flattered myself; and now I have been rash and impertinent to the only being——"

" No, no, don't say so;" and one single tear glistened a moment and dropped.

" Am I not then entirely indifferent ? Oh, Alice, if a lifetime of devotion could assure you

how sincerely I love you, give me the opportunity
of proving it."

Maidenly reserve and truth struggled for a
moment in Alice. She almost immediately saw
that they were consistent the one with the
other.

"It would be unkind to let you remain under
a wrong impression until we meet again. You
have surprised me into an admission. But we
have seen so little of each other. Surely a
solemn engagement, such as marriage, demands
something more than we see respond to it in
ordinary life. Can you bear to know me more
intimately, to see me, not as the *fiancée*, but as
the friend? every day should be dearer to us that
enables us to know each other as we are, and
not as we seem to be; not to awake some morning and find our idol broken and dishonoured.
Oh, how many are there in this world of ours
who would give millions to recall words spoken
in all sincerity, but which a false sense of honour
has led them to confirm! Our happiness—nay,
mine, if you will—must not be based upon such
an uncertainty. My whole heart, without one
single doubt, one single scruple, shall be given,

but it shall go hand in hand with respect and esteem. Are you satisfied with my honesty?"

"Yes, Alice, I presume I must be."

"Then let me say adieu to you here. Good-bye; God bless and protect you!" She held out her hand, smiled through her tears, and hurried from the room. Tom stepped into his carriage an hour or two later; his feelings were difficult to define: altogether he was a happy man.

Charlie remained at Brain Lees Manor, working with a savage determination only known to military candidates. It was thought desirable, about this time, that he should take a preliminary canter.

"Well, that's very good," said the Captain, one morning, after perusing an examination paper, of which he was himself profoundly ignorant. "Very good." The Captain was surrounded with books, and considered himself safe.

Casting a furtive glance at a Chepmell, he asked, in an important tone, "Who was Richard the Second?"

"Son of the Black Prince," said Charlie, who had really attained a considerable knowledge of

the history of England, by dint of hard work.
" Son of the Black Prince."

As this might be true or not, Old Armstrong
did not venture to contradict or assent, but immediately read from the book, " He thought it
unsafe to leave his nephews alive, and they were
secretly murdered in the Tower."

" Bless my soul, sir, what a mistake I made ! "
said a bright genius called Fothergill; " I thought
that was the crook-backed tyrant that Shake-
speare and Pickwick wrote about."

" Oh! ah! yes, yes, to be sure; I meant to
say Richard III., of course : what was I thinking
about ? "

" What was the Battle of the Boyne about ? "
asked Charlie in the innocence of his ignorance.

" Oh! the Boyne: the Boyne's in Ireland, you
know," rejoined the tutor.

" Yes; but what was the battle about ? who
fought it ? "

" Oh, it was a battle of parties—all those
battles were—Charles and the Roundheads. I
suppose your Latin's all right, Mr. Thornhill ? "

" Well, I believe I know enough to get some
marks above the minimum; but if you'll just run

through the grammar here and there, and then pick out half a dozen passages of Virgil —— "
Armstrong turned purple.

"Certainly; only, just now, suppose we go on with the English and the History." Just then in came Cantabs, who, if not very learned, had studied the art of cramming to some purpose.
"When do you go up, Mr. Thornhill?"

"Next week."

"You know your French?"

"Yes; I can translate it: not very good at the grammar—pronunciation horrible," replied Charlie.

"Ah, that doesn't signify. Latin?"

"Pretty fair: they flogged something into me."

"Euclid and arithmetic?"

"Three books, and all right up to quadratics."

"What are you most afraid of?"

"English," said the dunce: "they ask such odd questions."

"So they do. It's understood that nobody can answer them, excepting Max Müller, and he's a German. As long as you can spell well, and write a goodish essay, it will do. When you're doubtful about a word, write illegibly.

The prisoner has the benefit of the doubt.
There's your history and geography. They're
pretty good, I think. You'll get through. They're
sure to ask (just take a paper and put them
down) the descent of Victoria from James I.,
the sovereigns of Tudor—why they were more
despotic than their predecessors (I told you the
other day)—Marlborough's battles, Charles I.,
the Boyne, the four R's, Edward I. and III.,
and Henry IV. and V.; and remember a weak
king generally comes between two strong ones
—Strongbow, Simon de Montfort, Warwick, Cran-
mer, Melancthon, Walpole, Pulteney, Chatham,
Pitt, Fox, Liverpool, Burke (you'll have to write
a life of some of those in something under
twenty minutes), Aden, Delhi, Pulopenang, Mau-
ritius, and the military stations. Oh! and don't
forget the two Johnsons."

"Just tell us the difference now."

"One is Ben, and spells his name without
an *h*; the other is Samuel, and spells his name
with one. We'll look when they lived another
time. I'm hanged if I know. Come in."

"Second-post letters," said a boy in buttons,
not dirtier than they usually are. Why do not

the middle classes employ female labour for all domestic offices? Cleanliness, good-humour, and good looks, instead of dirt, idleness, and impertinence.

"Here they are," said Smith, the ex-Harrovian, taking them from the willing hand of the youth, who retired: "there's one for you, Fothergill, and two for Thornhill; and here's 'Bell's Life' of last week and 'Baily.'"

The party were instantly immersed in their letters or their newspapers; and Charlie's contained something which startled him.

The first was simple enough: it was from Sam Downy, and gave the latest intelligence in the fewest possible letters.

"HONOR'D SIR,

"The orse is well. We no all about it. Mum's the word, as we wont to ketch the rogues. More by-an-by.

"Yours to command,

"S. DOWNY."

The next letter was less expected: it was from his uncle, Henry Thornhill, from Pall

Mall. It also went the shortest way to its object.

"HAMMERTON & CO., PALL MALL.

"MY DEAR CHARLES,

"A friend of mine is very desirous of seeing you in London on business of importance to yourself. You will find him to-morrow before 10 A.M. at —— Street. After that at Mint, Chalkstone, Palmer, and Co.'s bank, East Gold-bury, City. Ask for Mr. Roger Palmer when you send in your card. I believe his business is very important to you. You can call on me afterwards if I can be of any use; and you will find your friend, Lady Marston, in town, who will be glad to see you. Adieu.

"Yours affectionately,

"HENRY THORNHILL."

"P.S.—Your father was a friend of Roger Palmer's, and once did him a service almost irredeemable."

That evening Charlie Thornhill was in London at his old quarters, Sir Frederick Marston's, where he underwent a little badinage on the subject of his military knowledge, but with a tolerable assurance that he was well worthy of his aspirations. Some men lead a forlorn hope, and others arrive at the Garter without it. Immortality is the lot of both.

Charlie was on his way to East Goldbury by twelve o'clock, and reached it about half-past one. He was not kept waiting. The little man sat in a comfortable inner room, with "The Times" over his knee, and warming himself by a good fire. He rose to salute Charlie, offered him a chair, and again sat down.

"Mr. Thornhill, I have no personal acquaintance with you, but your poor father was once the means of doing me so essential a service, at some risk and inconvenience to himself, that it will add sincerely to my pleasure if you can entertain the proposition I am about to make you, for my partners and myself. You'll take a biscuit and a glass of old Madeira?" Here he rang the bell. "How did you come?"

"I walked from Grosvenor Square." Roger Palmer gave a satisfactory grunt: it was indicative of energy, one of his virtues.

He then detailed to him, that from the large

Continental business they were doing, it was considered necessary to send a gentleman, not as a mere clerk, but almost as a partner. That a knowledge of French and arithmetic was necessary, and that German should be added to it: as, on the return to England, the youngest partner would have this part of the business to transact. That every facility would be given, as it was proposed that the gentleman to go out should be a bachelor, and reside in the family of the senior correspondent in Frankfort. That a handsome income, increasing according to circumstances, would be given; and that at the expiration of a certain term of years, the gentleman would be received as a partner in the house in England without any further premium or advance of money in any way. "In short," said the little man—and he had a struggle about telling or concealing it—"the income and the partnership will be yours by right, as I have myself advanced the needful. There, sir," said Roger Palmer, wiping his glasses, which had become a little dim, "there's a fortune for you, let me tell you, such as your ancestor may have had when he built Thornhills."

Charlie was so astounded by the unexpected nature of the proposal, that he could do nothing more than stammer out his thanks; but after a minute's hesitation the money part of the transaction seemed the most incomprehensible. He was anything but a man of business; but he knew quite enough to be well assured that such an offer was not obtained without a very large sum of ready money; such a sum, indeed, as it became him to reject at the hands of a stranger. He had a very proper pride, and the expression of it only endorsed Roger Palmer's determination in his behalf.

"Then you can't or won't see that obligations may arise between men which renders any future relations between their families quite extra-ordinary."

"I don't say that; but I have not lived, even to my age, Mr. Palmer, not to know that the obligation I place myself under to you is immense, and that I, at least, have no claim upon your bounty. There's my brother."

"Your brother, sir, ought to have enough; besides, the 'wind bloweth where it listeth,' and I desire to confer this, not as a present, but as a recompense for the work you will have to do, and the benefit we shall derive from it. Come, look on it in that light."

"I can't look on it in anything but its true light—a sense of obligation to a stranger. Excuse my saying so; but you know what I mean."

"You are proud, young man."

"Perhaps I am: it is a pride that I hope will keep me from doing what I can scarcely approve."

"Will you reserve your answer for three days, and consult your uncle and your best and most intelligent friends?"

Charlie hesitated, looked at Roger Palmer's face, and said, "I will."

"Then take another glass of Madeira, and adieu. Bless my soul alive," said the banker, as Charlie descended the steps of Messrs. Mint, Chalkstone, and Co., "I've more difficulty in getting rid of twenty thousand pounds than I ever had in making double the money."

Charlie called in Pall Mall. He detailed the whole conversation to his uncle.

"Can you translate French tolerably?"

" I think I can now."

" And do a sum in arithmetic ? "

" Certainly."

" And don't care about being a gentleman and a dependent for the next forty years ? "

" If coupled, it would be singularly distasteful to me," said our hero.

" And you came here to ask my advice with a view to weighing it ? "

" Most undoubtedly, my dear uncle." Charlie laughed.

" Well, you know, very few people do. Then you shall have it. Accept his offer."

Lady Marston and Sir Frederick dined at home. Charlie gave a succinct account of his visit in the City. " And now, Sir Frederick, what am I to do ? "

" I know the circumstances of the case, and you need have no scruples in accepting the partnership, or anything else. They owe their existence to your father's generosity and confidence. They were at their last gasp when your father, with scarcely a hope of saving them, and knowing full well their position, ordered every farthing he could command, besides a large sum which he borrowed, to be paid into their bank. It stopped the panic, and was the means of saving them. Accept it by all means."

"Frederick, nonsense—impossible! I've been down to the Horse Guards, and had a long chat with General Bosville; and he has promised me the first cornetcy in the household troops for Charlie. I shall break my heart if I don't see him in his uniform. I meant to have taken him to the drawing-room in your place—you know you dislike it—and now he's to be a banker. Never mind, Charlie, we'll have you in Parliament. It's absurd throwing away six feet two and so much common sense on a back parlour in Lombard Street."

"Then I'm still to be a soldier, Lady Marston," said Charlie, laughing.

"Well, that depends entirely upon your own inclination. If you like a life varying between Windsor and London, and all the pleasures which accompany a charming mess, the most intellectual conversation, champagne *bien frappée*, the idolatry of the queen's balls, parades, operas, clubs, and bachelorhood, by all means. But if you desire to put yourself in the way of doing a good work, or following a useful calling; of assisting your fellow-creatures; of becoming a really valuable member of society; and of bringing up a family after you, also to do the work properly that God sets them upon earth, then——"

"Ah! I see; I must go to Frankfort: so I accept to-morrow."

It was three weeks later in the year, and Charlie was to start on his new career very shortly. Arrangements had been made; and he was to open his life at Frankfort-on-the-Maine under the auspices of Herr Schlösser, Winkleman, and Co., and in the house of the former.

It was a dreary, drizzling afternoon when Charlie took his seat in the train for Dunham Heath Lodge, the residence of Samuel Downy. The crisis was come: in three days' time the race was to be run; and the horse was to be moved across the country to-morrow or next day. To-night the attack must come; and the information was to be relied on.

When Charlie arrived he found one of the boys at the station to carry his bag, with Mr.

Downy's favourite hack at his service. That
gentleman thought himself best at home under
the circumstances. When he reached the lodge
it was quite clear that good counsel had been kept.
Even Mrs. Downy herself knew nothing about
it. Her cap, or pagoda, or structure of whatever kind, was as brilliant as ever; her smile
as unfettered, her buttered toast equally good;
and the roast fowl and egg-sauce got expressly
for Charlie Thornhill, was not the cuisine of a
lady tormented with doubts, or ill at ease in
her mind.

"The horse looks beautiful, sir," said she.
"Lor! what dangerous work that steeplechasing
is, to be sure. One day here, another there.
Perhaps the poor thing may kill hisself, for
all his good looks. Downy often says he wishes
you gentlemen would stick to the flat. He says
that's a duty you owe to your country, but the
other isn't."

Downy was evidently big with the cares of
state; and well he might be. He had one
policeman locked in an empty stable on one
side, well supplied with beef and beer. Another
policeman in an outhouse on the other side,

also revelling in beef and beer, of which Downy himself had the key. And he had a third policeman, who had already partaken of hot gin and water, who was waiting in the little thicket at the back of the box in which Œdipus stood. All this had been done without Mrs. Downy's knowledge. What a clever fellow was Sam Downy!

"The time is to be midnight, Mr. Charles. We've made the boy safe; and as there's a little moonlight just then, we shall be able to see enough for our business." With this Sam Downy lit his pipe, Charlie his cigar; Mrs. Downy brewed some hot whisky and water, and then took to knitting, which shortly ended in a comfortable nap. Her better half soon followed her example. "My dear," said he, waking suddenly up, "I think you'd better go to bed;" and to bed she went.

At half-past eleven Sam Downy led his guest mysteriously across the 'yard. First he unlocked Policeman 1's box, then Policeman 2's box, proceeding cautiously to the rendezvous with Policeman 3. "There, sir, they won't show fight; but you'd better take the life preserver, in case of accidents. Rogues are always cowards."

They had been in their hiding-place not more than half an hour when they heard stealthy steps crossing an open patch of heath between the back of the stables and the country. Just then a cloud cleared away from before the waning moon, and they saw three figures, a boy and two men, crouching along the ground towards the yard, which was here open to the country. They crept slowly forward, passing within the shadow of the copse. Charlie longed to give a war-whoop and be at them, but was restrained by Downy, who rightly judged that the "ketching the rogues" was of the first importance. They allowed them, therefore, to continue their serpentine path along the side of the building, until they had turned the corner. Following them then as stealthily, they reached the angle in time to see the key applied to the lock. It turned without noise, and silently the two entered, whilst the boy remained without. At that moment a policeman appeared on each side; the boy became a willing prisoner; a very dim light scarcely shone in the stable; and Charlie,

Downy, and their companions had already their hands upon the latch, when a fearful scream woke the silence of the night, and pushing open the door, they beheld a scene of terror, which we reserve for another chapter.

.

.

CHAPTER XV.

PREPARATION.

"Shall I not take mine ease in mine own inn?"

THREE days later (and the winter was far advanced) the silent little town of Sedgeley was all alive. Sedgeley was one of those places that had been spoilt by a small aristocracy. A potent lawyer; a real physician with an Edinburgh diploma and nine daughters; a rector, who had been senior proctor; two medical practitioners; and a wealthy banker, who combined with his usury the advantages of chief linendraper of the place,—had set their faces against railway intrusion. It was not to be, and it was not. The consequence was that a thriving town, of four thousand inhabitants, with a roaring trade in penny whistles, came to nothing. With a melancholy sigh, as they met on the market hill, Judkins the watchmaker would expatiate to the new curate upon the former glories of his native town. He would tell him how twenty-four coaches, besides the great North mail, changed horses at "The Saracen's Head" every day. And indeed he said truly. There were nice little suppers, and whist and oyster parties, among the topping tradesmen, who were all well-to-do, for the place was constantly full of customers. There were snug dinners among the would-be aristocrats; and a great deal of jealousy when Sir Charles Trimmer invited the doctor, but forgot the lawyer, or *vice versâ*. It is but fair to say that they all came in turn; for as he was member for that side of the county, and politics in Sedgeley depended entirely upon the digestion, Sir Charles never forgot anybody who could enjoy a dinner at all, provided only that he possessed the requisite qualification. Now, however, all this was gone. The rail had been strenuously opposed, and in return had carried its passengers and its traffic, at four miles' distance, to the next market-town; and nobody seemed to care much about penny whistles—at least not sufficiently to come out of the way for them.

In the midst of all this dearth of riches or

amusement Sedgeley had become eminently dull, save on one or two occasions. Once a year there was a ball, and the principal room at " The Saracen's Head" was still in request. Whenever the hounds met within two or three miles (for Sedgeley was in one of the best hunting counties in England) all the idlers became busy. The landladies put on their best caps, and the ostlers were ready for any little odd jobs that might turn up on such an occasion. There might be a marriage once or twice in the year, which sent half a dozen extra people into the street, or to the church, and a funeral or two; but the inhabitants had no real taste for gorgeous solemnity. Sir Charles Trimmer might have died himself, and there would scarcely have been a respectable house to welcome his hearse and coaches. The present occasion was not of that sort. Something more than common brought down Mrs. Bustleton, with a wonderfully smart cap, at four o'clock, into the bar. It was neither a funeral nor a wedding that produced a ringing of bells, and a rustling of chambermaids and cherry-coloured ribbons, on so sombre an afternoon; and when Ramsbotham the saddler rushed

into the inn-yard with an old but very good-
looking saddle on his arm, to which he had been
doing something, quite a crowd of inquisitive
boys and lazy apprentices surrounded the gate-
way of "The Saracen's Head." However, Ramsbotham was not a man to satisfy anybody but a
customer or a creditor; and as to Tony, the
one-eyed ostler, he saw more and said less than
any man in Sedgeley. It was noised abroad that
there was one of the horses already in the yard.
The blacksmith had been consulted by the
groom, a very superior sort of person, it was
said, on the subject of a shoe, or a boot, nobody
knew which; but what shape, size, or colour he
might be was no more conjectured than if he
had been smuggled in in a bandbox. *Omne
ignotum pro magnifico.* Those who had not seen
him, and knew nothing at all about him, already
declared he must win; and not a few of them
backed their opinion that night at "The Cocked
Hat and Teapot," one of the most sporting little
cribs in the place.

"Well, Margaret," said Mrs. Bustleton, between mouthfuls of hot muffin to her sister,
"I wonder the gentlemen don't come in. It's

past five, and I'm sure they can't see to
hunt."

"P'raps they've gone the other way, you
know; and then they'd have a good ways to come
home. I heerd Tony say there was a good many
'orses already in; and I dessay the place 'ull be
quite full to-morrow."

"Yes, we must have the ordinary in the big
room, after the race. Sir Charles must take the
chair, and Mr. Thornhill and Mr. Dacre must sit
on each side of him, I suppose. The rest must
sit as they can."

"I thought the other gentleman, Mr, Somebody Brown, ought to sit the other side."

"Bother Mr. Somebody Brown, Margaret;
how you talk! He don't belong to the county.
We'll have Mr. Thornhill, and Mr. Dacre, if he
comes, or some of our own people, and Mr.
Charles Thornhill, all up at the top—— Lor!
there's a fly." And true enough, after paying
the fly and the driver, a tall, well-made man, in
rough coat and comforter, opened the door, and
stood unceremoniously in the badly-lighted corner
of the bar-parlour.

"Why, bless me! it's Mr. Charles," said Mrs.

Bustleton, colouring, and wiping her hands on her handkerchief.

" Right, Mrs. Bustleton," said he, stretching out a hand, and advancing to the fire; " let me warm myself a moment. I hope you are quite well, and the children ? "

" All well, thank you, sir; and Mrs. Thornhill, and your brother, sir ? We don't see so much of you as we did once, when you were boys, and used to ride over on your ponies. How's Miss Stanhope, too, sir ? I hear she's a great deal with Mrs. Thornhill. But there's your room ready, sir, with a capital fire : isn't there, Margaret ? "

" Thank you." But Charlie stood with his back to the fire, a little preoccupied. " And what time do we dine ? "

" Seven o'clock, sir. You'll take a biscuit and a glass of sherry, Mr. Charles ? "

" How many was dinner ordered for, Mrs. Bustleton ? "

" Six, sir, I understood. There's Mr. Tom, and yourself, and Lord Carisbrook, and Captain Charteris, and Mr. Stapleton, and some one else; but I didn't hear who. P'raps you'd like a cup

o' tea, sir?" Here Mrs. Bustleton made an attempt to squeeze the pot.

Charlie still looked down thoughtfully. "Is
Mr. Downy here with the horse?"

Mrs. Bustleton rang a bell, which summoned
the one-eyed ostler. "Tony, is Mr. Downy here
with Mr. Thornhill's horse?"

"No, mum—leastways, sir," said Tony, first
to his mistress and then to her guest, "No,
sir; he's coming this evening. The head man's
here."

"Send him to my room." And Charlie,
having picked up his overcoat and shawl, walked
out of the bar, ushered by a tallow candle and
bunch of cherry-coloured ribbons. "Come
in;" and William entered and the girl went
out.

"How did the horse come?"

"He never was better, sir. It's my opinion
he can't lose, if he don't make a mistake."

"But they do make mistakes sometimes—all
of them: however, that's as fair for one as the
other. How's the country?"

"A little sticky, sir; just suit the old horse, I
should say."

"I don't know: the mare's a thorough-bred one, and can stay."

"Well, Œdipus must be thorough-bred too, sir."

"He's not in the Stud-book. But how's the poor fellow?"

"Not so well, sir. He's been a bit delirious—talks a bit, sir. They couldn't keep his bandages on last night. The man's, you know, sir."

"But they don't think very badly of him?"

"Oh! no, sir; I didn't hear as they did." And here William scraped himself out of the room.

Charlie Thornhill looked at the parlour. It was a comfortably furnished room, with a good fire, and a dinner-table laid for six. He remembered it well. It was the room in which he and his brother met on the day of their eventful journey after the death of their father. He had been several times at the hotel since, which was only ten miles from Thornhills, but he had never been in that identical room till now. He looked at the pictures. They were the same. There was the famous American trotter, with the wonderful dog-cart, which looked like a wheeled spider. There was the late Mr. Bustleton, a short, red-faced man, in a dress coat and waist-coat, with his hands by his side; and staring at him—as he well might be—was a most extraor-dinary painting of his brown horse Solomon, the most striking points of which were the biggest head and the shortest tail in England. There was the Prodigal Son, with a hole in his hat, with nothing on but a shirt and a pair of knee-breeches, being welcomed by his father in a flowing wig and a court sword. His brother looks on in gloomy silence, while a groom in a blue livery leads a couple of saddle-horses up and down in front of the house. The butcher in the distance is sharpening his knife ready for the calf, which has not yet left her mother's side.

The door opened, and the same cherry-coloured ribbons appeared with a lamp. She was followed by a heavy footstep and the smell of tobacco. Tom Thornhill came in, and shook his brother by the hand heartily. Then came Lord Carlingford and Harry Stapleton.

"Charmed to see you, Charlie. How are the nerves?"

"All right, thank you. What sport to-day?"

" Very moderate. We found at Dodford, and
went down to Norton : it's a wretched scenting
country. We got on better terms with him
after crossing the Sedgeley road, but we lost him
at Driffield. I suppose Œdipus is all right,
notwithstanding the reports in town ? " said
Stapleton.

" What reports ? "

" Oh ! I don't know exactly ; but they offered
me three ponies to one against him yesterday.
I was such a fool as not to take it, thinking
there might be something wrong ; and then we
got the newspaper account of the skrimmage. I
suppose you had a horrid row at Dunham ?
They've committed them."

" Well ! yes, we had, rather. Tom, if you
fellows don't dress, we shall have the dinner
up directly." And they all four adjourned to
their rooms.

When they met again, Charteris and Baron
Hartzstein had joined them. They sat down
to a severe soup, fish, leg of mutton, and beef-
steak pudding sort of dinner. They washed it
down with some warm sherry, and ordered up
some claret. Tom Thornhill's name was suffi-

cient to get, at all events, the best the house afforded; and it may be remarked that gentlemen are the most easily satisfied, and the least preposterous in their requirements, of any class of persons. If I hear of an extravagant order in the way of dinner or wines at a plain country inn, I feel satisfied that, nine times out of ten, the consumer is a snob, and a savage delight comes over me that he is pretty certain to have everything as bad as it can be. Away from home the "mensa tripes" should be the rule.

"Capital mutton, Thornhill," said Lord Carlingford, with his mouth full.

"Yes: but not so good as the Southdown. We feed a few at Thornhills for ourselves."

"And they cost us about eighteenpence a pound," said Charlie, who had no opinion of amateur farming as a speculation.

"Who shows the ground to-morrow?" said Tom Thornhill.

"I do," replied Captain Charteris, "with Vincent of the 12th. He's coming with Robinson Brown in the morning. How much he's improved in his riding this last season or two! He's so much better a horseman than he was."

" By-the-by, Thornhill, you were going to tell us about the row at Dunham, and the attempt on your horse."

" Charlie knows all about it; he was there: not I."

It must have become evident by this time that one of Charlie Thornhill's besetting sins was his modesty. If he had to tell a story of which he was the hero, he made nothing of it. He loved a short cut to anything, and would gladly have said nothing more about the business. He seemed perfectly content that the horse was safe, and the perpetrators on the road to punishment.

" Let's have it, Charlie," said Tom. " I've hardly heard it properly myself yet."

" Oh! it's nothing particular. We found out that something was going wrong, so old Downy set a trap for the fellows, and caught them."

" But wasn't there something about Œdipus eating one of the fellows ? "

" Well! not exactly : Œdipus is quiet enough. It seems that Downy had got a new boy, who mistook his orders. The boy ought to have changed that savage horse of Martin's—Homicide they call him—to an empty box: but he made a mistake, and put Œdipus into the empty box, and Homicide into our horse's place. They're not very unlike; and when Downy went round he never saw the mistake."

"Well! but what happened?"

" Oh! nothing particular," said Charlie, helping himself to sherry; "we followed the men into the box without their knowing it. The horse was loose; and before we could get into the place, he rushed at one of the fellows, knocked him down, and seized him by the side with his teeth. Luckily, Downy was there, and got him off, by one or two violent blows on the nose; but the fellow was picked up half dead. He has broken several ribs, and his side is terribly lacerated; but I hope he'll get better. The other fellow is remanded, and will be committed, of course.

" Where's the wounded prisoner? He won't get off, will he?"

" Certainly not. There's a policeman sleeps in the room. But he can't be moved; and Downy's man says he's not so well to-day."

" So nothing at all happened to your horse?"

" He wasn't in the box at all."

" What a fool I was to let those three ponies slip, to be sure; " and the recollection seemed to make a profound impression on Stapleton, who asked for the claret. " And what are they going to do with Martin's horse, the Homicide ? "

" Make a watch-dog of him, I should think," replied the dunce of the family.

Tom Thornhill rang the bell, and ordered some cards and a backgammon board. Before long he and his friends had thrown some mains; and now that the Devil had once got possession, he armed himself to keep it.

" Come, Charlie, one main ? "

" No! no!" laughed Charlie; " not I. You know I never play. Besides, I'm going to bed." This was a wise measure for a fool.

" Bed! what, at ten o'clock ? Smoke a cigar: here's a capital one."

" No, thank you: smoking at night's a bad thing for the nerves; and I've got all your money on my shoulders. You'd better let me go to bed."

" He carries Cæsar and his fortunes. Well! good-night; and good luck to-morrow."

"Good-night." And then the play went on more and more furiously. And these bosom friends forgot each other, and gloated over their own interests. There is a substance and there is a shadow—of generosity. The substance is the habit of mind, the shadow is the impulse. The one costs much, the other little: but the former shines with but little lustre before the world. Perhaps the world's eyes are not yet attuned to seeing in the dark. Be that as it may, the gambler has a reputation for generosity. He has the impulse, and grasps at the shadow. The substance is too hard for him. Not all this, but something like it, ran through Charlie Thornhill's mind as he heard the silence below him, only heightened by the clang of the dice.

"Ruined! irretrievably ruined!" said Prodigus, as he turned from the inquirer to conceal his emotion.

"Are you, by——? I'll lay you a hundred to twenty of that," returned his most intimate friend.

A gambler never understands ruin till it stares him in the face, and then he strives to stare it out of countenance. We all harden in time:

but there's no fire like the dice-box. Wife, child, self, soul, are all too light to put in the balance with the turn of a card. Oh! Alice, Alice! what an intuitive knowledge of the world for one so innocent and so young!

CHAPTER XVI.

THE WALK OVER, AND THE RACE.

"Si sors ista dedit nobis, Sors ipsa gubernat."

CHARLIE slept well (it was his custom) when
he got rid of his waking dreams about gambling.
There was always one figure which occupied the
principal part of the picture. Tom was altering :
not to him, nor to his mother. Still he had
become capricious in his moods. He wanted
constant society : before, he liked it, but was
equally cheerful without. It seemed as though
he were putting a good face on something, but
did not feel it the less. Why in the world didn't
he marry ?

They were all off to look at the ground. Four
miles from Sedgeley, on the Croppington road,
equally convenient for Robinson Brown, who had
a box for the season, not half a dozen miles off,
and for the Thornhills, who lived in the county,
ten miles from Sedgeley. Charlie drove out in a

fly with Charteris, Lord Carlingford, and his
brother. He intended walking the course. Vincent and Robinson Brown were at the public
before them, with a couple of hacks. Lord
Carlingford's man had horses there for the
others. Three accepted them, but Charlie
adhered to his opinion and his legs. He
was essentially a shooting-boot style of man.
Robinson Brown was patent leather all over.
A man's character almost always resembles his
boots.

The ground was already marked out with
flags. It was plain and broad, as another path
is said to be. A good four miles of it.

"The riders will keep the flags to their right
hands, if you please," said Vincent, who was an
excellent judge of such matters. "It will be
found a fair hunting country. You can go anywhere to the left of the flags, so that you may
have a choice of places."

Two or three gates let the horsemen in, whilst
Charlie surveyed them on foot with a critical eye.
The first four or five were good hunting fences,
with nothing remarkable, and as easily seen
from a pony as any other way. Then came a

cramped place—the ground a little raised before taking off.

"Not to be ridden at too fast," said Charlie to himself; "and to be sure to get close up to it."

"That's an easy fly," said Robinson Brown, from his hack. "A donkey could do that."

"Here's the water, Charlie. It's a fair jump everywhere; but the banks are rather higher in some places than others above the water."

Charlie stood between two willows, and measured it with his eye. "What's the width, Tom?"

"Width? Oh! 'pon my word, hav'n't the slightest idea. You'd better ask the depth, Charlie. It looks quite big enough to get into."

"Not with Œdipus. I think I could jump it myself."

"Very likely," said Carlingford; "but that won't win the match. Come on. There's nothing but grass up to here, and the next field is the only bit of plough in the race." And on they went, smoking and laughing, till they came to a ridge or furrow of more than ordinary inequality. It was almost like the sea, and "A man overboard!" would not have sounded very

mal-apropos in it. The way out of this difficulty
was over a good stiff double post and rails.
There was no room to land between; and it
must be done at a fly.

"A most unmistakeable cropper," said Charlie,
again to himself, "out of such a field as that."

Robinson Brown was chatting away with his
friends, and surveying the scene with considerable *nonchalance*, seeing that he was going to
play a prominent part in the drama to be enacted
shortly. Either he had great confidence in himself, or his mare, or his luck: for the course was
a decidedly stiff one, and nothing short of a
fatalist could have regarded the last field and
fence with indifference.

"Brown, that's a big 'un," said Wilbraham, a
good sportsman, and one of the leading men with
the county hounds.

"Wather; ya-a-s. A-should say, a wegular
yawner."

"Deucedly like himself. Near relatives. I
hope they'll agree." The speaker had backed
the mare for a hundred, and called the owner's
attention to an obstacle or two, which seemed
to escape him. "What did you think of the

water? I suppose the mare's pretty good at that?"

"Water? Oh? ah!—the bwook. Ya-a-s: to be sure."

"Yes, the brook. You saw it, I suppose? Because you'd better canter back if you didn't. That's all."

"Ya-a-s, I saw it. I call it a waŧine. It's a jump."

"Jump; indeed, it is a jump!" added his backer, in hopes of reviving either his spirits or his attention. "It's not unlike a family vault. "You won't get out in a hurry, if you once get in."

"Jump or vault, Weluctance will do it, Basset,

> 'Wise from the gwound like fwather'd Mercuwy,
> And vaulted with such ease—'

Your hundwed's safe enough." And on they went. Beyond this the fences were fair hunting fences—timber occasionally; a thick bullfinch here and there, interspersed with a little child's play; and a second arm of the same brook, but by no means a formidable. place. They were nearing the finish, and had passed about five-and-twenty fences, when a flag, placed on a high bank over which it was impossible to see, attracted universal attention.

"Hallo, Charteris. What's this?" shouted the owner of Œdipus.

"That's a bank," said the Captain. "A new line of rail coming."

"Then I hope it will break before these fellows get to it; that's all."

"If they don't like it, they can go round. But I'm going to explain for Vincent and myself. We were ordered to pick four miles of hunting country, and we agreed that that bank was an obstacle which might present itself whenever the hounds run across here. Besides it's as fair for one as the other. If Brown don't object ____"

"What do you say, Charlie? Capital place to see it from."

"Excuse me, Thornhill," said Vincent, "but you don't understand that if they don't like it they can go round. It only extends to the next fence, and on the other side of it there's a regular passage through, which brings them into the straight running again. It's rather out of the way, but not above a hundred yards or so."

In the meantime the whole party rode to the top (the ascent was not very steep) to inspect the slope on the other side. It was an awkward-looking drop. The ground shelved at considerably less than an angle of forty-five degrees. It was about thirty feet high, and, being covered with a stunted herbage, looked slippy in the extreme. It was about one hundred yards shorter in distance, and there was a saving of one very easy fence in the corner of the field, immediately under the bank. As there was an alternative, to be easily adopted by either or both, nothing more was said on the subject. The remaining fences had been inspected and approved of; and as the course was arranged so as to form a semicircle, it was not a difficult one for the spectators. A large pink flag was carefully placed in every hedgerow, and the top of the bank was so conspicuous an object that it served for an excellent landmark for at least a mile beforehand. The time was getting on—one o'clock—and the start to take place at two—or as soon after as gentlemen can get into their breeches. They all turned towards the little village inn from which they had started, where carpet-bags, portmanteaus, horses, flys, grooms, and the various types of the fine old English farmer, had collected in great number.

"Well, Charlie, what do you think of the course?" said Tom Thornhill, whilst his brother pushed himself into a thinner and tighter pair of breeches than usual, and proceeded to pull on the very neatest pair of tops possible.

"Very good course. That's a sticker, that bank, you know. I suppose we shall both go round," said Charlie.

"Most likely. If there had not been a road on the other side of the fence, I should have objected."

"I'm glad you didn't. It is a hunter's course, after all; and I dare say many a horse would go down safe enough. Shy us that boot."

"Don't put that jacket on; here's a purple and white stripe," said Tom again, tossing him one from a chair-back in the room.

"What an odd fellow Tom is! Who'd have thought it? I wonder whether he likes the girl. I once heard Alice Dacre say something about

———" And Charlie began to brush his back hair, preparatory to the cap.

"Now, Charlie, come on : there goes Robinson Brown." Tom was flushed and preoccupied when they got down; and Charlie began to think it was an object to him to win this match, independently of the original bet.

He went down stairs slowly, as men must in boots and spurs, covered over with a light great-coat of approved fashion. He found half the county ready to shake hands with him. It was a non-hunting day, and everybody within distance had come to see it. The betting was even—if anything, a turn in favour of Œdipus : a sort of reaction, after his knocking out. Or was it Charlie's jockeyship?

The crowd below was thick and anxious; and the heroes of the day were not likely to be more than an hour late at the starting-post : in fact, it was only half-past two o'clock, and they were already on their hacks, and starting for the post. To judge by the crowd that accompanied them, and the crowd that was already gone before, steeple-chasing was in the ascendant in the neighbourhood of Sedgeley. All the farmers' wives and daughters were there in flys, four-wheelers, dog-carts, and carts taxed and untaxed of every description. There were the county members, with their wives and their sons and their sons' wives, one in a barouche, the other, the younger and more dashing, in a mail phaeton : his private brougham, too, was drawn up behind him near the winning-post. The member for Croppington was there too, on a clever hack ; and the Master of the Hounds. Upon this occasion they were on the most friendly terms : as a rule, politics divided them. A goodly company planted itself at the brook—decidedly the most sporting lot—and I must confess there is something sublimely pleasant in seeing another man get a ducking. It beats all dry falling into fits. At other misfortunes one grieves, as applying the Aristotelian theory to one's self, that it may be our own case. But whether we are so satisfied of deserving to be hanged, or from what cause soever I know not, the risk of drowning never affrights us in the case of a brother sportsman's mishap. So, many hoped for a catastrophe, and remained at the brook to see. The post and rails was also a pet

place : it numbered some of the ladies, who are
always kindly and tenderly placed at the spot
most favourable to accident. Besides the county
families, the members of the neighbouring hunts,
and the farmers and sporting tradesmen, there
was a strong London division, who were pecu-
niarily interested in the affair. In a word, for a
private match, not supposed to excite particular
interest out of the county, it was the most
marvellous success that had been known for
years.

We have already stated that Tom Thornhill's
colours were purple and white stripe; Robinson
Brown sported all white. Œdipus was a magnificent dark-brown horse, of great power; but he
has been already described. Reluctance was a
racing-looking mare, a good golden chestnut,
showing vast speed, and low and long. They
were both capable of crossing any country, and
their condition almost unexceptionable. The
horse for choice in this respect; the mare a little
too fine. She had, however, a great turn of
speed.

They are off! Charlie would willingly have
made running at his own pace : he could depend

upon his horse to stay, and he suspected a turn of speed in the mare. Reluctance, however, was too fresh to be steadied at once, at least by Robinson Brown, and the running to the first fence was in his hands, I might say out of them. Charlie watched him, as did many more. Away they went, the mare lurching at her bridle, and her rider sitting a little uncomfortably, to all appearance. Now her head was down, now up, and his hands were evidently full. Œdipus was fresh, but was held together in a manner that told him pretty plainly he had his master on his back. Charlie had the inside, and steered close to the flags. He remembered every fence, and knew pretty well where to have them. Robinson Brown was not a bad man on a good horse, a hunter; but the mare was fresh, and he was up in his stirrups, and obliged to go faster than he liked. The first fence was nothing extraordinary; but he went at it faster than he ought to have gone. Charlie sat down on his horse closely, just easing his quarters, and as near the middle of the saddle as need be. His power over his horse was manifest; and Œdipus gave him a good hold of his head. "Steady!"

said he, as the horse became excited by seeing the mare in front, and hearing the crowd behind. Crash, smash, flop, went the amateurs in the rear. They were well after him, but not anxious to show him the way. The white gates, which ran nearly parallel with the line, were of great service to the ladies, and to not a few of the gentlemen. The fourth field was ridge and furrow, and the mare began to settle. Robinson Brown is no great favourite of ours; but he was not a fool in the saddle, and began to be more at ease. He still had to look back for Charlie, who kept his own line, at six or eight lengths behind. They were coming to the cramped fence, with a suspicious bank in front. "I thought so," said the Dunce to himself; "steady, Œdipus!" and he dropped his forelegs just in the right place, and landed well, as Reluctance pulled her hind leg out of the ditch, and shot Robinson Brown a little too forward to be elegant. There was no fall, however, and they were again side by side. "Well saved," said the crowd. "She's a quick 'un," thought Charlie, "and won't fall for want of a leg to spare." The horses now went stride for stride by one another; and the riders eyed each other. Like two of Homer's heroes, they look for a hole, but the joints of the harness were well riveted ; no weak spot was perceptible. The crowd was silent enough. No incident, no fun, nobody down yet. The ponies and hacks had turned aside and sought a shorter and safer cut to the water or to the goal. The Master of the Hounds, Lord Carlingford, Tom Thornhill, and a cavalry officer or two, were within half a field ; the rest sadly tailing. The pace had been good ; but both horses held their own. The line of willows appeared in the distance, and crash went the rotten wood of an old pleached fence, with the ditch on the taking off side. The mare cleared it all, and was a length into the next field before Œdipus. "Bravo ! that's the way to do it," said a warm-hearted tenant of old Robinson Brown, from the bough of a tree, who owed a half-year's rent, and wanted a new barn ; "the young master wins for a hundred." Nobody took him : there was nothing on his bough up to that mark. " I'll lay you five shillin' on the squire's brother, Measter Chanticleer," said one of the Thornhill party. "Lor ! bless you," added the old sportsman, "see how he handles his

horse : he's a savin' him for the water; we ought
to ha' been theare." In the meantime they
were nearing the brook, and a low fence and
ditch brought them into the very field. Charlie
marked his spot at once, and Robinson Brown,
in advance about six lengths, diverged a little to
the left, looking at what he imagined to be
an easy place. It was not so big, but the
ground was low on the taking off side, and
the water was shallower, having fallen over
an artificial dam. The mare put back her
ears, and went round like a shot. The first
refusal; but no blood drawn. Robinson Brown
held on by the bridle. Charlie kept the upper
ground, and squeezing the old horse, sent him
at it, where the bank was highest. The place
was wide, but sound, and he landed well on the
other side. The white handkerchiefs went up in
the carriages, and a little buzz of applause, but
the interest was too deep for a shout. Just then
he heard one, and hoped his competitor was in.
Robinson Brown was just getting on his legs, the
mare was already up again; he had fallen the
right side. He took a pull at Œdipus, and
looked at the mare. She was pulling double,

and seemed all the fresher for her fall. Brown
looked positively cheerful, and Charlie never
liked him better than at that moment. He really
could ride, and had plenty of nerve. It was only
even betting still. It was anybody's race now,
and they were entering the ridge and furrow
field before coming to the double post and rails;
Charlie well in advance, and Œdipus going up
and down like a pony. Reluctance surely could
not go over ridge and furrow like that. But she
did; and Robinson Brown raced to catch him.
"Not a symptom of distress in either," said
young Dacre, as he sat on his mare, to some
ladies in a carriage beside him; "but Charlie
looks like winning. What a horseman he is!"
The taking off was not good, and Charlie knew
it; so catching the horse tight by the head, and
putting all his heart into it, he sent him at the
most favourable place he could see. There's
never a great deal of time to think when once in
the air, and a faint shriek was the first intima-
tion that he had smashed twenty feet of stiff
timber, and was down. "Lucky I held him
tight," thought our hero, as he jumped on to his
feet, almost as quickly as Œdipus, and, shying

the reins over his neck, threw himself into the saddle. He had just time to see that the mare had done it all safely, and was well to the fore, when he set his horse going. His situation was precarious, and he knew it. Wherever Charlie went he carried his head with him, even if it were not worth much. Three-quarters of a mile from home, the fastest horse of the two in front, by about a hundred yards, and heaps of other people's money on the event. There were five more fences, and whoever was round the bank first must win. Round the bank? there is but one chance for it, and it must be done. Reluctance still went on with the lead, and though the horse never slackened his pace, the mare didn't come back, as Charlie intended she should have done. He began to shorten the distance by a trifle. Yes, by Jove! she's getting shorter in her stride, and here's the plough. It's a sticker at the end of three miles and a half; and Charlie looked for a furrow full of water. Robinson Brown kept straight on. Flop, flop, flop, went the horse; but still he gained; and he entered the next field about sixty yards behind the mare. And there's the bank, right in front, which separates them from the winning field by a single fence. Crowds of people lined the ridge, even to the right of the pink flag they extended. What will the rider of Reluctance do ? As he neared the obstacle he looked back, then he felt his mare, then he looked at the people. "It's all over," thought he ; " he can't do the bank, and I won't risk it." He turned away to the left, and steered straight for the gap in the corner, that let him through to the opening in the proposed line of rails. As he reached the gap, Charlie steered straight for the hill; holding his horse firmly, and jogging him up the ascent, the people in suspense cleared a road, and shouted applause. Straight over the bank he went. Slide, slither, slide ! but with his head perfectly straight for the winning chair, Œdipus came towards the bottom of the descent ; and just as he looked like falling, within ten or twelve feet of the bottom, Charlie jumped him into the course. At the same moment Reluctance, in full stride, appeared beyond the edge of the bank within forty yards of the horse, and right abreast of him. " It's a race ! it's a race ! " shouted the people. And it was. But Œdipus was straight for the fence before him, and the

mare came diagonally towards it. They both
jumped it together, but the mare had shot her
bolt; and as Charlie turned round to look at her
he shook his horse gently for a couple of strides,
and cantered in a winner by about six lengths.
Time eleven minutes and a half, and Robinson
Brown quite pumped. "That's a d—d good
animal, Jane, dear, and I'll give you five hundred
for her," said the Hon. Smoker, from the judge's
stand.

"You'd better wipe those scales," said Charlie;
"they're all over dirt, and these colours of Tom's
are quite new."

As he was riding slowly off the course, an open
carriage ploughed its way solemnly through the
grass; it was stopped near Charlie by the crowd,
and the well-known voice of Lady Elizabeth
Montagu Mastodon, of whom we have lost sight
for a time, was heard in congratulation.

"The first time we ever met, Mr. Thornhill,
was after a steeple-chase, but I little expected we
should ever meet at one. However, my friend
Edith Dacre is too much of a sportsman to stay
away; and as Mr. Mastodon is not enough of a
sportsman to come, I have been doing penance.

Let me congratulate you on your success. If it's worth doing at all, of which I'm very doubtful, it's worth doing well. I suppose you've made a fortune."

"You forget that I never bet," said Charlie, taking off his hat to Edith, and longing to get round to that side of the carriage, but wondering, at the same time, what everybody would think.

"Bless me! no. Your brother does that for both of you. We've not seen him for an age."

Charlie apologised for Tom and himself. They had both been away, but he would ride over to-morrow or next day to take leave. He was going to leave England for some time. Charlie looked at Edith's face as he spoke, and he saw something which gave him hope.

When he got back to Sedgeley, Mrs. Bustleton had a note for him. Sam Downy had been summoned to the room of the wounded gipsy, at the moment he was about to start for the steeple-chase. He begged Mr. Charles to come over; there was something to divulge, and he would tell it to nobody but Mr. Charles Thornhill. He could not live; he was injured internally, and in his spine. The letter begged him to come quickly.

He went as fast as posters and the train could take him to Dunham Heath. It was too late; the poor fellow was dead. Tom Thornhill followed in the morning. They went into the chamber of death, the two brothers. The woman drew aside the sheet from his face, and there, in the Gipsy George, and the Whitechapel Dog - stealer, lay the mysterious visitant to Gilsland.

"And he was there?" said Tom.

"Assuredly."

"But he came to warn me, and refused to take my money. I didn't believe his story."

"You see it was true, sir; but lor'! we'd made it all right before he turned king's evidence."

And then they heard from Mrs. Downy, and the nurse, and the police, of a mixture of names, which seemed to startle, as a roar of very distant thunder: a storm that had passed away—Kildonald, and Burke, and Squire Thornhill, and the meeting on Bidborough Heath—a terrible night, and never mentioned amongst them; buried, forsooth, in profound mystery; and now, for the last time, as it seemed, in the grave. How soft, placid, and beautiful the face of the gipsy was, as he lay in his long last sleep! His matted hair clustering round his white forehead, and his long eyelashes lying on the cheeks, from which all colour had at last fled. How little symbol of his noisy and criminal existence remained behind! Have we buried all his evil with him, or no?

Charles Thornhill rose from a seat in the drawing-room of Fossils Thorpe Park, a few days later.

"Good morning, Lady Elizabeth. I must say good-bye," said Charlie, looking round the room, however, as if he missed something which ought to be there. It was getting dusk, and he had a sharp ride to Thornhills before him, as he justly remarked.

"Miss Dacre will be sorry to have missed you; though, as she returns home next week, you may see her at Gilsland before you leave England." Here her ladyship held out her hand cordially, for Charlie was a favourite, and said, "You must ring for yourself, or walk round to the stables; I get so very lame, Mr. Thornhill."

Charlie preferred the latter, and retired. In crossing the hall, Edith Dacre met him; she had just returned from a walk in the park. I know

nothing so becoming to a girl's face as the roses
gathered from the fresh air of a fine winter's
day. Summer roses carry the seeds of their own
failure in the heat that produces them; but hiber-
nal bloom tells of health, vigour, animation, life.
So thought Charlie at the moment Edith recognised him; and he stopped, absolutely perplexed
by her beauty. It was nothing new to him to be
perplexed, it is true. Still he floundered and
faltered, till she fairly turned round, and walked
towards the hall door. It opened on to a terrace
which, at any other time than a raw winter's afternoon, might have invited a walk. Her bonnet
was still on, and very becoming.

"My dear," said Mr. Mastodon, half an hour
later, "who is the gentleman whose horse was
just now being led out of the visitors' stable?"

"Just now? If you mean an hour ago, it was
Charles Thornhill."

"Of course it was; the white-legged chestnut:
but he is only this moment gone."

"Then he'll have a very cold ride of fourteen
miles, and scarcely be in time for dinner. I suppose he's been admiring something."

"But it's pitch dark."

" Perhaps he admires somebody. Did you see Miss Dacre, my dear ? "

" No, Lady Elizabeth. That's an imprudent idea. He hasn't a shilling."

" He may not be the worse for that. I don't like monied men—at least they're not all like you. Besides he may make a fortune—one of his ancestors did." Her ladyship was partly in his confidence. After all, he was not such a dunce as they tried to make him out. To be sure, Tom was the genius, and that always makes a difference.

CHAPTER XVII.

" Now leave to talk of love,
And humbly on your knee
Direct your prayers unto God,
But mourn no more for me."—*Ballad*.

IN one of the wings of Gilsland were three rooms
en suite. They belonged to the Misses Dacre.
There was a common sitting-room, shared by
both, and a bed-room opening from it, on either
side. It was at their option to share the same,
or to retire to separate rooms.

They had dismissed their maid, and sat in
demi-toilette before a fire which lighted up the
warm-looking carpet and winter curtains. Edith
had that day returned from Fossils Thorpe Park,
and was resting her head on her sister's shoulder.
There was no lamp, but a small flat candlestick
was, so to speak, thrown into shade by the
fitful, but fine glare of the Derbyshire coal fire.
There were tears gathering fast on her lids, and

her cheek was flushed—at least as much as could be seen from the luxuriant folds of her rich brown hair.

" Oh, Alice dear, what a weight of happiness in all this uncertainty!" said she, as she let a tear fall upon her sister's hand.

Alice kissed her kindly, and then said, " But why make a weight of it, darling? You must love him dearly. Who could help it? "

" But papa and mamma. Dear mamma; what a disappointment!"

" Come, courage! Edith. I know papa better than you. Act as you ought to act. Have no secret from them. All will go well."

" Ah! if I had but your courage, dear Alice. But you have no secret such as I; you have no trouble, dear. So it's easy enough for you to advise." And here Edith was getting a little out of temper, and becoming by consequence unjust.

" And how do you know that I have no secret and no trouble, Edith?" said her sister, colouring to the temples, but making a bold effort to look her sister in the face. It was unnecessary; for Edith only buried her face deeper in her sister's bosom, and sobbed the louder. "I have a secret and a trouble such as you." Edith raised her head, and her tears ceased to flow: surprise had dried them. Alice did not need to bury her head whilst she made the confession of her love. "I fear no confession to my dear father, nor to my mother, darling; but I fear to make it to myself. I have not told them what he said to me, nor what I said to him, for I have not accepted him; and it is his secret as much as mine. But I tell you; and you must be cheerful and happy yourself, and help me to be so. Mine is a worse burden than yours, dear: yours will be light enough in time, but mine will grow heavier every day." And here the stronger leant upon the weaker, and took comfort from their mutual helplessness. They did not think with the prince of classic dramatists that

"Τό τοι διπλάσιον ὦ γύναι, μεῖσον κακόν."—*Ajax. Soph.*

"Then you don't love him, Alice, as I love Charlie?"

"Why not?"

"Because you don't trust him."

"Does a mother love her child less because

she will not trust him when wandering on the brink of a precipice ? "

" Then reclaim him, as the mother reclaims her infant."

" You shall have no secret to-morrow, dearest. We'll both confess together. To-night, God bless and direct us both." But they did not separate that night.

The scene changes to Thornhills, and it is after tea.

" Nonsense, Emily ! why in the world should you be in such a hurry to marry him ? You always talk of it as an universal panacea."

" It would be in his case. And how are you to know anything about it ? "

" I think I know quite as well what's good for him as his mother, at all events," rejoined Aunt Mary. " You've always spoilt him : and now you want to punish him for your self-indulgence." Aunt Mary was given to warmth of temper as well as heart, and made considerable grimaces, according to her custom, at such times.

" Spoilt him, indeed, Mary Stanhope. That's rather good of you, who never allow him to be contradicted."

"Well! he is coming here to-morrow; and, from all I hear, he's not very well disposed to take his medicine." Here she groaned and yawned, and put her hand to her side. She was always an invalid on these occasions.

"He'd be much oftener here, if we asked some one to meet him."

"He would if you filled your house with sharpers, and gamesters, and——"

"I shall write and ask the Dacres to-morrow: he was at Oxford with Edward Dacre, and I dare say he'll enjoy the pheasant shooting. As Charlie won't be here, they'll want another gun."

"Charlie's worth a dozen of him, and much fitter to be married than he."

"I hope it will be to Miss Robinson Brown, unless you intend to support them." And here Mrs. Thornhill shook out the voluminous folds of her dress, and prepared for further combat. But Aunt Mary would not go on. She gaped, and looked at her cousin with considerable temper. Her sallow complexion and dark eyes were lighted up with a spark of uncommon fire; and, ringing the bell unceremoniously, she retired for the night, without a salute.

"How stupid Mary Stanhope is! She thinks she knows everything, and is always giving her opinion about Tom's extravagance. I'm sure, if he only got a good wife, he'd be the best husband alive. I shall certainly ask those Dacre girls for the shooting week." Here the soliloquy ended; and, ringing the bell, she followed the example of her cousin Mary, and went to bed. She thought, too, that a mother's prayer would not hurt him.

CHAPTER XVIII.

RETROSPECTIVE.

" Et sa présence, ainsi qu'à vous,
  M'est un cruel supplice."--MOLIÈRE, *Mal. Imag.*

THE pleasure of writing a novel has its draw-
backs. The necessity for going back, as the
only means of getting forward, is exceedingly
troublesome. But it must be done. We seem
almost to have taken leave of some of those with
whom we opened our story; and we never knew
the value of our friends, nor our creations, till
they seem to have left us for ever. This is just
the case now. We would willingly leave every
one to tell his own story in his own way, more
by ethical than by historical development : but
before we can do so, we must retrace our steps.
Just to make the place tidy we will sweep up the
crumbs.

After the strict investigation, and hopeless
mystery, which succeeded the assassination of

Geoffrey Thornhill, Kildonald had disappeared from the scene. Circumstances had placed him in so questionable a light, that many persons were not without their suspicions that he was directly or indirectly concerned in that affair. Those, however, who were best informed, entirely exonerated him. The whole circumstances, the intended duel, his return to Henry Corry's house, and information of the murder, the improbability of the thing altogether, and his uniform explanation, served to acquit him in their eyes. His absence from England immediately after the final dismissal of the case could easily be accounted for. He could show his face no more amongst his former companions. The Clubs, St. James's, Newmarket, and Melton, were henceforth closed to Kildonald, as thoroughly as if he had been the archfiend; and there were none behind as bad as himself. He had committed the unpardonable offence of being found out. The Jockey Club pronounced on the case with a zeal and honesty of expression quite edifying, and made such a raid amongst the suspected of the betting fraternity, that no one was found out again until very nearly the end of the season.

However, Kildonald got his ill-earned money
from Burke, and retired to that Paradise of
Sharpers, the Continent.

Kildonald was a man of quick impulses : some
generous ones ; and not all bad.   His errors had
been those of education ; strong temptation ;
and an incapability to resist.   The loss of his
property, and the ties he had contracted—his
false position in the world, and the evil influence
of a man like Burke, who, as we have seen, held
him by some secret power—were the rocks on
which he split.   He had never felt his position
before this time : he had done much that was
dishonourable, but it had never recoiled upon
him, as his present disgrace.   If we were all
found out, I wonder whether we should most
despise or pity one another !

Geoffrey Thornhill's death affected him very
seriously.   It made him think ; and the Tyrol,
not then so *recherché* as it has since become, is
a great place for solemn reflection.   Kildonald
was not hardened, depraved ; but he was not one
of those erring, but fine minds, which can make
reparation at its own expense, or take vengeance
upon itself.   So he carried with him the money,

the price of his dishonesty, and lived quietly, cheaply, and unknown, not far from Saltzburg. He thought highly of his self-immolation, and the mausoleum in which he had buried himself alive. There are many like him. His reasons for this seclusion were manifold, and did credit to his head and heart. It was not expensive: it was out of the world: was not unlike the wilder parts of Ireland, on a larger scale; afforded good, but inexpensive education for his children; and was not so unpleasant to his wife, as a life of exile might have been.

When he left England, his wife, Norah Kildonald, whom he loved very sincerely, had decided upon going with him. During his hours of prosperity she had borne his absences without complaint, under the impression that he was happy. In a season of adversity, when the world frowned, she insisted on her right of comforting him: what woman does not?

She came: and the household of Mr. and Mrs. Kildonald was small, but gracefully administered —after the fashion of woman. She brought her son and her stepdaughter. She had never inquired further than the fact, which she had learnt piecemeal, that her husband had made an early and imprudent marriage. Kathleen was the sister of Gipsy George.

For a length of time they grew old together. But by degrees Kildonald pined for the world, not exactly of London nor of Paris; but for an approach to its suburbs. He had forgotten his peccadilloes, as easily as the world had forgotten him. Besides, to be boxed up in a Tyrolese village, for Norah and Kathleen never to see a soul, and the boy, who wanted to see something of society before he went into the Prussian service! His father preferred it to Austria. Norah sighed : she knew the meaning of "seeing a soul." Kathleen was glad of any change that promised to break the monotony of a very dull life : Kildonald himself felt like a returned convict, or ticket-of-leave man—on his best behaviour, but with an unmitigated taste for housebreaking, with violence.

" What's the matter, Arthur ? you look tired," said his wife kindly.

" Tired ? I'm ill, Norah. This place doesn't agree with me. I can't stay here any longer. I should like to get back into Germany."

After some discussion, Frankfort was fixed upon. Here, in an obscure street, not far from the Jews' quarter, they rented a small flat. Kildonald was pleased for a time : then a run to Wiesbaden or Homburg was easy, and on one or two occasions he came back smilingly—occasionally a reverse happened. His means of subsistence to you and me was a mystery. Norah believed in the old Kildonald estate. The facts are simple.

Some money he had. It did not last for ever. Two years after his expatriation he heard of the losses on the Kildonald property, by reason of the non-completion of the sale by the Thornhills. He certainly had had no money, nor was he receiving the rents of the estate. He applied in Cork, by means of friends, for a statement, a settlement, a something. He could get neither of the two first, and there were reasons why he could not employ law. But he got the something. He got money, when he wanted it, doled out at intervals, by Burke. It seemed that Burke was receiving the rents, and claimed the estate, by a mortgage upon it for the greater part of its value. He was unwilling to foreclose ; and

he was not a man to be forced into explanations,
at any rate by Kildonald. To say truth Kildonald cared but little for anything, if he could
gratify his passion for play, which had only lain
dormant for want of opportunity. Each year
since their absence from their cottage in the
Tyrol had seen them on a downward course.
Norah tried hard to stem the tide; but the devil
was too strong for her, and ruin was running its
course. Norah was a woman; and as her husband
sunk in her esteem, he seemed to have risen in
her love. What could she do? She began to
teach in Frankfort. An English governess, resi-
dent in the town: so charming a manner; so
sweet a face; always a smile to cover that aching
heart, could not fail to make friends. But teach-
ing is not highly paid anywhere, least of all
in Germany: a few florins monthly, to help her
boy, who was at Düsseldorf, or Kathleen, who
was not old enough to help herself, found their
way to the gambling table. But Kildonald was
not himself—there was always some evil influence
behind him: silent, unknown, but secretly felt.
Norah felt it, knew it: Arthur was so changed:
it was Ireland over again, with the weight of

years added to its pains. And so we have brought them down to this present time : and the evil influence is again upon the stage.

There had been great doings at Mainlust. It was a fine evening in autumn, and the gardens had been full to a late hour. There had been music and *weissen wein*, and *rothen wein*, and smoking and flirting. It was very late, and all good and quiet citizens of the free city had left long ago. There lingered some ladies of the old town, some noisy Fuchs from Heidelberg, and two or three officers, finishing their last bottle. They were not all. At a corner of the gardens, not now so well lighted by the coloured paper lamps as half an hour previously, sat two mysterious-looking persons, smoking, not drinking, and conversing in low tones. They were not Germans, still less Frenchmen ; and the contrast between themselves was even greater than that between them and their late comrades. The one was stout, short, vulgar ; without beard, but portentously whiskered ; and singularly over-dressed. The other was tall, thin, pale, and iron-grey. Singularly aristocratic-looking, prematurely old : he wore a drooping moustache and large beard. He was remarkably quiet in his dress, and but for a certain nervousness would have been equally so in his manner. It would have been difficult to have recognised in him the former *Gandin* of London, and the finest horseman of his day. They rose at the same moment. The one saying, with a vulgarity of Irish accent somewhat rare in society, "I wouldn't have known ye anywhere, Kildonald. Sure, you're changed, man!"

"And you, not at all. I should have known you, Mr. Burke, if I'd met you in the streets of Pekin or—or—Cork."

Burke winced under the allusion to his native city, and was silent for a minute—"how much did he know, or how little?" thought he.

"Shall we be going?" at length said he.

"With pleasure," rejoined Kildonald.

They took their way from the gardens, as the last waiter extinguished the last lamps and carried away the last empty bottle, along the quay. It was a warm night, and they walked slowly, distrustfully, without the cheerfulness of friends, or the energy of open enemies. They were useful to each other, mutually suspicious, and mutually fearful.

"Which is your way to-night?" asked Kildonald, assuming an air of coolness, and turning a cigar in his mouth.

"To the Mayence railway."

"You have come the wrong road—it lies the other way."

"I have an hour to wait for my train, and will accompany you home."

"Impossible! my lodgings are not — not exactly——"

"If there's a chair to sit down upon, I'm content; faith, I know what roughing it is, since we knew one another before."

"But it's—there are reasons——"

"Pooh! pooh! what, an old friend, Kildonald? Come, bedad, we must talk the matter over: between us, sure, there's no ceremony."

Kildonald stopped at a turning which led on the left towards the Römerberg and the Cathedral; he hesitated a moment, and seemed suddenly to make up his mind : then said deliberately, "You forget that Mrs. Kildonald is with me, and my daughter—let us turn towards the station."

"And pray, sir, have you forgotton to whom you're indebted for that same lady, whom you call Mrs. Kildonald?" Kildonald turned pale; he felt it, and his companion must have felt it too; for he as suddenly added, "but there, man, let us talk of something else. What about the young Englishman? when will you come to 'the Mount?'"

"I cannot assist you further than I have done," said Kildonald.

"Then thank you for nothing; you've found our fox, which any one might have done; but I can't kill him alone," rejoined the other.

"Without hounds, I suppose you mean to say," and the tone in which Kildonald spoke had a bitter irony in it.

"Perhaps I do : but at least we hunt in couples —I share the risk——"

"And take the whole of the profits. You must find another dog to bear you company in this matter, for I cannot."

"Say—will not. But, come, Kildonald, you throw fortune away from you at the very moment she is at your feet. Listen; there's enough for us both to be got out of this wealthy Englishman, this Carlingford. He plays high, and eagerly. He wants no persuasion, has no skill, not even common prudence. Sure you or I may profit by our knowledge: we've bought it."

"And I have paid for it, Mr. Burke: it costs you nothing. Have you one soul to drag down to infamy besides your own ? have you a wife, a son, a daughter?—yes, I repeat it, a daughter; for she's as dear to me as the rest—who might live to curse the infamy of a father who sold them all to misery and vice, because—because——"

"Because he wouldn't see them starve. Where's the infamy? We play as thousands more. We are successful. Why not? Are we accountable for the losses of a young fool who thrusts himself into the way of danger ? Come, you take this too seriously. What is it ? The whole of these rascally pettifogging foreigners live by play. What they call play—some half-dozen florins a day. The young Earl does not care for the tables: they're not quiet enough, nor high enough for him. He likes hazard. Lord Carlingford can bleed enough in one night to—what shall I say?—to enable you to—ay!—to

pay me the whole of the debt on the Kildonald
property. With good nursing it can be made to
pay twice its present income ; and you may return
to Ireland, be yourself again, and leave it to your
boy——"

" Saddled with his father's dishonour," and the
sigh was one of decreased resistance.

" If it was so, bedad I think he wouldn't
refuse the offer," said Burke, who saw that he
had made an impression, and became less guarded
in his brutality.

" What ! " said the other, hoarsely, " with the
education of a gentleman and a soldier——"

" Which are you speaking of ? "

" Ah ! stop, Burke ; true, true. You remind
me, cruelly, very cruelly. But—another time ;
not now, sir—how hot and suffocating the air is."
And here Kildonald took off his hat, and wiped
his brow. He stood still, looking on the waters
of the Maine, as it ran rapidly towards the Rhine.
In that moment a thousand contending thoughts
flitted through his brain. He tried hard to collect them—to arrange them. He thought he
ought to resent something, and yet there was a
cogent reason for not offending. He tried to be

dignified, but a strong sense of degradation, a
weight of previous necessity, kept him down.
At last he said, "I'm not well this evening; to-
morrow, or the next day, we may meet again:
but pray leave me now."

"Then dine with me to-morrow. No. The
day after, then. Come; and bring Mrs. Kildonald and your daughter. It will do them good
to run over to the Mount." (The Mount was
the name given to a cottage in which he lived
half a mile from Wiesbaden.) "I'll ask Lord
Carlingford."

"Yes; the day after. There; good night."
And, as if fearful of further parley, he turned
round, disappeared up one of the narrow streets
leading from the river.

Burke turned away, and returned by the river-
side. "I have him safe enough," thought he.
"With Kildonald's assistance we shall manage
Milord admirably. He's not half out-at-elbows
yet. Lords never know when they are ruined.
There's but few of 'em been through my hands."

The street up which Kildonald turned was one
of those very old, picturesque parts of Frankfort which have been enlivened by Prout and

Roberts, but which, without the bits of bright
green, blue, or scarlet, never seen in the original,
are brown and dingy-looking enough. The
houses overlap one another, and the upper
stories overhang the lower, so as to render it
very artist-like, but dangerous and dirty in the
extreme. The confusion of his mind, the con-
flicting hopes and fears, his anger, and the necessity for restraining it, battling in a not-over-
strong frame, had a very painful effect upon him.
He had not recovered himself, and, though perfectly conscious of it, he could not prevent himself from reeling. Once he stopped short, as if
about to fall; but he recovered himself again,
and proceeded towards his own house. It was
in a mean back street, not far from the cathedral
—between that and the river. At that moment
he felt a hand on his arm, and a good-natured
voice said, " Excuse me; I followed you from the
quay, and seeing you were a countryman, and
evidently unwell, I thought I might offer you an
arm. Lean on me."

The assistance was very timely, and too kindly
offered to be refused. Kildonald took the stranger's arm; and, after a silent walk of a few

minutes, he halted at the corner of the street in
which he lived. He thanked the stranger grate-
fully for his assistance.

"And are you certain you require no more?"

"No, thank you, I feel better. A sudden
faintness overcame me. Besides, I'm at home.
Adieu; and many thanks for your kindness."

"I wonder how much of our conversation he
heard?" thought the last speaker.

"Well, that was a dismissal, at all events,"
thought the good Samaritan. "Now who, in
the name of fortune, is he? and who was the
man I met by the water-side. They were after
no particular good, by the little I heard. This
fellow looks like a gentleman. Confound these
streets, how dark they keep them! A Jew's eye
ought to have been a bright one." However, he
was soon in the "Zeil," and let himself into a
handsome house with a latch-key.

The next day Kildonald was ill of paralysis;
and it was many weeks before he left his room.